# Mrs. Brodie's Academy for Exceptional Young Ladies

*Theresa Romain*

*Shana Galen*

MRS. BRODIE'S ACADEMY FOR EXCEPTIONAL YOUNG LADIES

Copyright © 2018 by Shana Galen and Theresa Romain

THE WAY TO A GENTLEMAN'S HEART

Copyright © 2018 Theresa Romain

COUNTERFEIT SCANDAL

Copyright © 2018 by Shana Galen

Cover Design by Kanaxa

Stock Images by Shutterstock and Period Images

All rights reserved. Except for use in any review, the reproduction or utilization of this work in whole or in part in any form by any electronic, mechanical or other means, now known or hereafter invented, including xerography, photocopying and recording, or in any information storage or retrieval system, is forbidden without the written permission of the author.

All characters in this book have no existence outside the imagination of the author and have no relation whatsoever to anyone bearing the same name or names. They are not even distantly inspired by any individual known or unknown to the author, and all incidents are pure invention.

## *Acknowledgments*

We'd like to thank Karlene Barger for the title of this anthology. We'd also like to thank Abby Saul for her role in production, Kanaxa for the cover, Joyce Lamb for copyediting, and Sarah Rosenbarker for proofreading.

Shana would like to thank Theresa and the Shananigans for their input on the title of her novella.

Theresa would like to thank Shana for being a fabulous writing partner on this project. And as always, Theresa thanks Mr. R and Little Miss R for being her HEA.

## *Contents*

The Way to a Gentleman's Heart............................9
Counterfeit Scandal.........................................139

# The Way to a Gentleman's Heart

## A Novella

### Theresa Romain

## Chapter One

*April 1819*
*London*

"Scale of dragon, tooth of wolf," chanted Marianne Redfern as she kneaded dough for the next day's bread. "Witches' mummy, maw and gulf of the ravined salt-sea shark…"

She trailed off when she noticed her assistant, Sally White, looking at her with some alarm. "Did you…are you making a new kind of bread, Mrs. Redfern?"

*Mrs.* The honorific always made Marianne smile. She'd never been wed in her life, but as cook at the exclusive Mrs. Brodie's Academy for Exceptional Young Ladies—and a young cook in addition, at age twenty-eight—she was due the status and protection of a fictional husband.

"Just amusing myself, Sally," she reassured the girl. "Shakespeare's got the right rhythm for kneading, but you won't see me feeding our girls any of those ingredients."

She liked the wayward sisters of *Macbeth*, the three prophetesses who drew a king's notice when they predicted his rise—then his doom. There was a certain man whose face she liked to imagine in the dough when she punched it. She didn't want to bring Jack Grahame to his doom, exactly, but when a woman had once had a lover's notice, it was difficult to be cast aside.

Since then, she'd become a bit wayward herself. Though she had no magic but that created by a stove or an oven, carried out with grains and meats and vegetables. Bespelling only for the length of a bite or a meal.

It was enough. It had become enough.

Satisfied with her dough, she turned the worked mass over to Sally. "Divide this part into rolls for the second rising, this into loaves, and cover it all. Put it in the larder so it will proof slowly. It'll be ready for baking in the morning, and the young ladies can have fresh rolls for breakfast." At Sally's nod, Marianne patted her on the shoulder. "Very good. I'll be on to the sauces."

Sally had been cook's assistant in the kitchen of Mrs. Brodie's Academy for only a week, having moved up from the post of kitchenmaid when Marianne's previous assistant married the butcher's son. Marianne could teach any girl who wanted to learn, and indeed Sally did, for she had dreams of heading her own kitchen someday. Katie before her had been a fair worker, but her heart hadn't been in cookery. She'd wanted the kitchen post only because she was in love with the boy who brought the meat. For three weeks they'd called the banns, yet Katie had said nothing to Marianne of her plans to marry. As soon as the parish register was signed, she sent for her things—and that was that, with no notice.

Love, love. It made people so deceptive. Yes, it was a good match for the girl; as wife to a butcher's son, she'd never go hungry. But even better than making a good match was knowing a body could take care of herself, come what might.

That was the purpose behind Mrs. Brodie's Academy for Exceptional Young Ladies, and it applied to everyone, from the headmistress herself to the youngest scullery maid. Along with the usual French and drawing, the students learned forgery and how to hold their own in a fistfight and God knew what else. The servants were welcome to take the same instruction after their daily work was done, if a teacher would agree to it. And for a little extra pay—no one could accuse Mrs. Brodie of being an ungenerous employer—most of the teachers were willing indeed.

Marianne had arrived here eight years before, new from the country and without even rudimentary skills in the kitchen. She'd worked as kitchenmaid and then assistant under a fine cook, Mrs. Patchett, until that good lady had retired to Devon to live with her son and grandchildren on a family farm. From Mrs. Patchett, Marianne had learned how to use and care for knives, how to clean and chop produce, how to choose the best fish and fowl and meat, and above all, how to provide three meals a day for seventy-five teachers and students, plus the army of servants who kept the school running smoothly.

It was difficult work, and hot, and physical, and sometimes dull. And Marianne would do it forever rather than return to Lincolnshire. After eight years here, two as the head of the kitchen, she had never been stronger, faster, more skilled. She could split a sheep's head, knee a presumptuous man, and stir a sauce of stock and cream to keep it from splitting—all at once and without turning a hair.

She had made something quite fine of herself, though the Miss Redfern who had first come to London might not have been so impressed. That young woman knew nothing but silk and song and embroidery and manners.

Marianne glanced at the clock that beamed from the corner. Eleven o'clock already, and most of the preparations were finally done for dinner at six. That was the main meal for the students; their midday repast was a simple one of breads and meats and cheeses, eaten between their lessons. She and Sally could assemble that in another hour, and the footmen would arrange platters for the young ladies in the refectory.

There was just enough time to begin a pastry for tarts before Marianne started the slow-simmering sauces. Tarts would be more special than a simple dessert of fruit and cream, and the young ladies deserved a treat now that they were nearly done with their spring term. The early apricots Marianne had bought that morning were fine and sweet; she could make do with them. It still smarted that she'd failed to win the first strawberries of the season from a greengrocer who'd wanted to charge the earth. Not that they'd have made tarts enough for all the students, but she had a weakness for strawberries.

"Sally," she called. "I need you to work with the apricots once you've stowed the bread."

When the answer *yes'm* came in reply through the open door of the larder, Marianne turned to her book of receipts and looked up her favorite ingredients for a tart pastry. How much flour ought she to remove, substituting almonds? One part ground almonds to ten parts flour might do the trick, enriching the delicate flavor of the apricots with melting sweetness.

She peered into the canister where she kept the nuts, pounded to powder and ready for use. Almost empty! She cursed. It was one of Sally's tasks to keep a good supply of pounded almonds, but if Marianne didn't direct her, the younger woman couldn't be expected to remember every detail of their stocks. They needed another kitchenmaid to fill Sally's old role, and soon. Mrs. Brodie's annual Donor Dinner—Marianne couldn't help but think of it in capital letters—was in a fortnight, after the term ended, and there was no way a single cook and assistant could prepare two formal courses and assorted desserts for one hundred people.

Well. She'd recruit the scullery maids to chop and peel if she had to, and she'd jug and stone and jar and press as much ahead of time as she could. And for today's tarts, butter alone it would be in the pastry, and that would keep the cost of today's meals down too. Mrs. Brodie was never mean with her kitchen staff, allowing Marianne all the budget she liked. Even so, the gentleman's daughter who'd once spent several pounds on a single bonnet now measured out ground almonds in cautious spoonfuls and haggled to the ha'penny over the price of lettuce or fish. When it wasn't her own money she was spending, she was more responsible with it.

Again, the face of Jack Grahame came to mind, and she wondered fleetingly if he'd felt the same about his father's money. The money that had been needed, and that she'd had none of, and that had split them apart.

Money. Money. Money. This time, there was no dough for her to punch.

So she turned her thoughts to the tasks before her, the ones she did every day. She checked the joints slowly roasting in the ovens, confirming that the coal held out. She pulled out the ingredients for the sauces she'd make for dinner; she sifted shelled peas in her hand and approved the amount. These could be cooked shortly before the dinner service. They'd boil in a flash and be finished with fresh cream and…something else. Something surprising and flavorful. Chopped shallots maybe, fried crisp in lard and scattered like beads over the top. Yes, that would do well.

Now back to the tarts. Sally had finished with the bread, and at the other end of the long worktable, she was settled with a great pile of apricots. Clean, cleave, discard the stone, set aside. The halved fruits went into a huge bowl, piling up quickly.

"You've a good rhythm for that work," Marianne told the younger woman. "Thinking of Shakespeare? Scale of dragon, tooth of wolf?"

Sally blushed. "Little Boy Blue. It's a nice old rhyme, that. My mum taught it to me and my sisters."

Marianne smiled as she dug her hands into the flour and butter, now coming together smoothly. "I have sisters too. Haven't seen them in a long while, but I remember learning those old rhymes with them."

*But where is the boy who looks after the sheep?*
*He's back in Lincolnshire. Do not weep…*

No, that wasn't right. That wasn't right at all.

A knock sounded then on the door to the tradesmen's entrance. The kitchen was a few rooms away, but the servants' quarters were quiet at the moment. The footmen were likely upstairs, while Mrs. Hobbes, the housekeeper, would be making the rounds of the students' chambers as the maids were cleaning them. She'd a keen eye and would come down hard on any maid who hadn't done her work well. Her husband, the old butler, had grown hard of hearing in recent years. If he were polishing silver in his pantry with the door closed, he wouldn't hear a Catherine wheel going off two feet away.

"Are we expecting another delivery, ma'am?" Sally asked with mild curiosity.

"Of kitchen goods? Not until I do tomorrow's shopping." Marianne eyed her butter-covered hands, then the pile of apricots her assistant had left to split and prepare. "I'll answer that door. Back in a moment, Sally."

She wiped her hands on her apron and wound her way past the servants' stairs, their hall, and the housekeeper's room. Unfastening the door to the area, she lifted her brows, prepared to scold a lost delivery boy for interrupting her work.

But it wasn't a delivery boy at all.

Her startled brain took a moment to understand the sight before her. The thoughts went like this:

*Oh! It's a man.*

*A handsome man.*

*He looks familiar. Does he work for the fishmonger?*

*No, he's not holding fish. Strawberries! He got those strawberries I wanted of the greengrocer. Look at him holding them, juicy and red, in that little basket. Does he work for the greengrocer?*

*Of course not. I'd have noticed him there.*

*No, he looks like…like…*

And then she knit all the pieces together, and her jaw dropped.

"Jack," she said faintly. "Jack Grahame. Why are you here?"

"Marianne. I brought you strawberries," said the man she'd loved and hoped never to see again.

When he held out the little basket, she took it, bemused. She looked from the strawberries to the face of her first lover, her only lover, dressed as fine as ever and handsome enough to be in a painting. Then back at the basket. And then she remembered that her hands were greasy from butter, her apron had a bit of everything she'd cooked today upon it, and her hair—her long dark brown hair that he'd once run his fingers through, lovingly—was sloppily confined under a cook's cap, and her cheeks were flushed from the heat of the ovens.

Ah, hell. If one's long-ago love showed up unexpectedly at one's door, it ought to be at a time when one looked one's best. But Marianne was a cook now, and a cook was what she looked like.

She lifted her chin. Closed her hands around the basket of strawberries. Did he remember she liked them, after all this time? Bright as rubies, and she'd rather have them than gemstones.

"Well. Thank you," she said with as much dignity as she could manage. "Is that all? As you're here, you know I'm working as a cook. And since you were always a bright fellow, you must guess I've got to get back to work."

"Since you asked, I'd like to come in and speak to you. Do the strawberries win me a little of your time?" His brows were puckish, his mobile mouth always at the edge of a grin.

So he *did* remember. "Time enough for you to say you're sorry for keeping away so long." She tried not to sound as soft as she felt, but her own words betrayed her.

The humor on his face melted. He looked at her with grave gray eyes and said, "I'm not here to apologize, Marianne. But I do want your forgiveness."

He'd always liked her eyes. In a face as calm as any cameo painting, her changeable eyes had betrayed her true feelings. If he read their green depths correctly now, he'd caught her by surprise, and she wanted to flay him alive.

But she also wanted to pop those strawberries into her mouth.

She teetered between the two urges. The strawberries made the difference; Jack could see the moment when they decided her. Her fingers tightened on the basket.

"Come in, then," said Marianne in a harassed tone. "I've not a moment to spare till the afternoon, but if you want to watch me at work, that's your business."

The tone he'd expected; her turning on her heel, he'd also been prepared for. The sight of the academy's servants' quarters as she led him along was something new in his experience. A winding space with whitewashed walls and timber beams, it was divided with shelves holding every sort of household ware and cleaning supply.

The kitchen space was huge, much bigger than the equivalent room at his Lincolnshire estate, with a stone fireplace large enough for a man to step into if it hadn't been crossed by an intricate arrangement of spits and hobs and hooks. There was a wall of ovens set into brick, atop which a long cooking surface—of some kind of metal, maybe?—held pots larger than any Jack had ever seen. They were practically washtubs, able to hold gallons of soup, and from them, savory smells issued forth.

At the center of the room was an immense table, wood-topped and scarred by cuts from kitchen implements. From a seat at one end, a young blond woman wearing a tidy white cap peered at Jack. A mountain range built of apricots surrounded her.

"Mrs. Redfern? Is everything all right?" she asked in an accent of pure Yorkshire. It made Jack smile—not only to hear one of the northern accents that sounded like home to him, but to hear Marianne addressed as *Mrs.* It must be an honorary title, for he knew she'd never married.

He couldn't say the same. Which was part of why Marianne wanted to flay him alive.

"Miss White," Marianne said in a crisp, formal tone. "Permit me to introduce an old acquaintance of mine. Mr. Grahame."

"Grahame?" The girl perked up. "That's a Lincolnshire name, isn't it? Are you related to Lord Irving?"

"I'm his poor relation," Jack admitted. "Or so his lordship thinks of my branch of the family. We've got land, but no title. His bunch of the Grahames have both, which as you know, makes them better."

The kitchenmaid, he presumed she was, giggled at this.

"Are you indeed still poor? I thought you'd taken steps to remedy that." Again, that crisp voice from Marianne. She had plunged her hands into a giant bowl of…he had no idea what it was. It looked like flour and butter, but the way she was squishing it to bits, he couldn't imagine what it would become.

"No, I'm not poor anymore," he said, feeling almost reluctant to say so. He reminded himself of the words he'd rehearsed so carefully: *I am not here to apologize.* He couldn't, for if he did, it would make the last eight years of his life nothing but a wrong decision, a wrong path traveled.

A boy in livery ran in just then. "Any of the ovens needin' coal, mum?" he tossed over a shoulder as he lay hands on a full scuttle.

"They're all right, Evans," Marianne replied, "but check again in a half hour, please." When the boy bobbed his head, then tore from the kitchen as swiftly as he'd entered, she turned to Jack with a faint smile. "Oh, for the energy of the young. Now I see that if you've something to say to me, there will be other ears about."

"Can you walk out with me?" As if he were twenty-two again, and she twenty, and he were calling on the neighboring landowner with an eye to the eldest daughter.

"I can't get away for a minute until luncheon is tidied away. However…" She eyed the mountain range of apricots. "How are you at cutting fruit?"

"I've used a knife before, if that's what you're asking, and I can tell stone from flesh. Why?"

"That'll do." Her faint smile turned wicked. "Sally, I'll need you to see to the young ladies' luncheon today. You'll find everything you need in the larder and the meat safe."

"Oh, mum!" The young woman—surely she could be no more than twenty?—popped up from her seat, eyes wide and eager. "Do you mean it? Cut it and plate it and everything?"

"The footmen can help you with the plating, and they'll take the dishes upstairs to the refectory. But they'll be yours to command." Marianne added as if an afterthought, "I'll just need you to prepare everything in the servants' hall."

"Oh. Not in here?" The girl's light brows knit. "But shouldn't I finish with the apricots?"

"You can't do that and arrange luncheon." Again, that wicked smile. "Mr. Grahame wishes to visit a kitchen? He can become a kitchenmaid for a while."

Miss White—Christian name Sally, Jack now gathered—looked as if she found this highly entertaining. Shaking out her skirts, she practically danced from the long kitchen. Off to put together a luncheon for a school full of, as the academy's name told Jack, Exceptional Young Ladies.

"If her enthusiasm is anything to go by, she's a good assistant to you," Jack observed once they were alone.

"She is, and better every day." Marianne rubbed the doughy mass in the bowl between her hands. "We've a little less than half an hour before the boy returns, and you've all those apricots to cut up. If there's something you want to say, say it now. While you work the knife."

"I like a woman who knows her own mind," Jack decided, settling himself in the chair vacated by Sally. "I'm not intimidated by things like apricots, you know. They're little and cute. Not frightening enough to scare a fellow away."

"I'm not trying to scare you away." Wiping her hands, Marianne scattered flour over a few square feet of her giant worktable, then heaved the mass of dough onto it. "I'm trying to get on with my work. And I sincerely hope your 'little and cute' comment was *only* referring to apricots."

"What else could I have possibly been referring to?" he said blandly. "I don't see anything else little and cute in this kitchen."

No, Marianne had never been *cute*, nor was she exactly *little*. She was of medium height, and he thought her striking, a woman of frank eyes and a straight nose and a full mouth and a stubborn chin.

Now she used that full mouth to frown at him. "First you don't intend to apologize. Then you say I'm not little and cute. You could have kept all that to yourself. You could have stayed in Lincolnshire."

"Probably."

"Then why the devil are you here, Jack? Are you trying to win me over again?"

He hadn't prepared this answer; he spoke on instinct. "I'm not apologizing because I can't say I'm sorry for the life that brought us to this moment. And I didn't say you're little and cute, because you're so much more than any word I could apply to you."

For a moment, she only stared. Then she sighed, her shoulders relaxing. "So glib. As always."

"It was rather good, wasn't it? And it's even true."

"Cut the apricots," was all she said, though to his ear, it sounded like, *Fine, you've won a bit more of a reprieve before I boot you out.*

Instead of cutting an apricot, he reached for a strawberry from the basket. They'd been ungodly expensive, probably forced in a hothouse, but he'd never forgotten Marianne's yearly delight when strawberries appeared for a scant few weeks in the kitchen gardens.

Taking the large knife up in his other hand, he carefully cut the little green leaves from the top of the fruit.

Marianne was watching him, lips parted. "What are you do—"

He held out the strawberry to her. She looked down at her hands, covered in flour and what he realized now was pastry dough, then returned her gaze to Jack. He kept holding out the strawberry to her.

Maybe, he realized, he had come to apologize after all. But not in words. In strawberries.

At last, she relented, opening her mouth so he could pop the berry between her lips. The gesture was familiar, friendly, intimate—yet strange. They'd done this so many times in the past—first as childhood friends feeding each other berries and later as lovers sharing the sensual fruit. Now they were strangers.

But some things remained the same, such as the bliss on Marianne Redfern's face as the taste of a strawberry spread across her tongue.

She allowed herself that moment of pleasure, then snapped back to work. It happened so suddenly Jack was caught by surprise.

One second, her eyes were heavy-lidded and her lips berry-wet. The next, she was taking a rolling pin to the pastry dough before her.

He set down the knife, leaning forward. "Marianne, don't you—"

"Cut the apricots." Under her rolling pin, the dough became an even, flat sheet. "And did you know you're still wearing your hat?"

He cursed, then tossed it onto a chair beside him and raked his fingers through his hair. "How do I look? Handsome?"

"Wash your hands," was all she said as she turned to a shelf and took down a stack of tart cases.

He grumbled his way to the pump in the scullery, then back. Seating himself again, he took up the knife and applied it to the first apricot. "You used to think I was funny."

"I did. You used to think I was a lot of things." Roll, roll, cut, cut, press, press. A tart shell took form in one of the cases, then was set aside as Marianne took up the next round of dough.

How could he explain what she'd meant to him? She'd been more than a first love. She had been his companion for as long as he could remember. He'd wanted to marry her. When he was twenty-two and she twenty, he'd asked her, and she had agreed as if it were the most natural thing in the world.

But Helena Wilcox had had money, and the Redferns hadn't, and if the Grahames hadn't got money at once, they would have been ruined. Tenants lost, lands fallow, dowries drained. All

Jack had needed to do was wed the merchant's daughter, and he'd spare everyone.

Everyone but himself and Marianne.

In the end, the marriage had lasted only six years before illness took Helena. Marianne knew she died, because she sent a proper letter of condolence—not to Jack, but to his mother and his eldest sister, Viola. She'd done the same when Jack's father had died a year later. Only recently had Jack put off mourning clothes for them both.

"I thought you were everything," he said slowly. The knife cut the pale flesh of the apricot, revealing the stone. If it weren't for the stone, the fruit could go right into the tart. But there was always a stone.

He cut another, and another, a whole pile of them as tart cases stacked up under Marianne's quick hands. Finally, she replied. "I loved who I thought you were. I've missed that man."

He couldn't argue with that. "I miss that man too. Do you know, you're the only person who ever loved me without thinking of how I could serve, or who else I could become?"

She stared at him. "Surely not."

Which was not a denial. Her disbelief warmed him, that not only did she grant she'd loved him just as he was, but she thought someone else must have too.

"Not that I'm aware. Anyway. That's why I wanted to find you. Not because I want anything from you now, but to remind myself that once, it was enough for me to be Jack Grahame."

"You said you wanted my forgiveness."

He cut more apricots, wanting to finish this small thing she'd asked of him. "True. I do want that of you. I couldn't have acted differently eight years ago unless I were...not me. If that makes sense?"

"Yes, it makes sense." She slid the bowl of cut fruit toward herself, eyed the quantity, then added a few fistfuls of flour. "If I had to marry to save my family from ruin, I'd probably have done it too."

His heart skipped upward, lightened. He tossed the last few apricot halves into the large bowl. "Then you don't blame me?"

She added sugar to the fruit. "Who else am I to blame, Jack?"

When she put it like that... "If you've the need in your heart to blame, then no one. There's no one to blame but me." A sapskull with a pile of stones before him, his hands covered in juice.

"I don't know," she said, and he drank in every flicker of emotion that crossed her features. "I hold you responsible for your actions. For the way you dropped me so quickly. But do I think it was the wrong choice? No, I don't suppose I do."

"Then you forgive me?" He was holding his breath.

"There's a distance between *don't blame* and *forgive*. I'm not ready to step across it yet." She took a breath. "But if you've two weeks to give, I could use a kitchenmaid."

He laughed.

She raised a brow.

"Oh. You're serious? A kitchenmaid?"

"I'm serious," she said, worry creeping into her tone. "I can't take any more time like this, to talk with you and eat strawberries. I'm behindhand with today's custards and sauces, and there's a great dinner to prepare in two weeks' time for all sorts of people who help fund the academy, and we're short on staff since Katie left, and—"

He popped another strawberry in her mouth. "Don't eat the leaves."

She bit the red fruit from the top, still in mid-word, and questioned him with her big green eyes.

And because he'd never been able to deny her anything but his hand in marriage, he agreed.

## Chapter Two

Before sunrise the next morning, Marianne was up and dressed and ready to work. She lit lamps in the kitchen, greeted the maids as they bustled through the servants' hall, then entered the larder to retrieve the dough Sally had placed in the cool room the day before. The buns and loaves had risen slowly and were now beautifully puffed, ready to pop into the ovens and feed a hungry academy.

Still adjusting her cap and apron, Sally joined her a moment later and helped to carry the dough from the larder into the kitchen. Marianne then peered into the adjoining rooms to look for Jack, but in vain.

She hadn't spotted him upstairs in the servants' attic quarters, either. Though, of course, he hadn't moved into the academy upon accepting the temporary post as her kitchenmaid.

Instead, he had the nicest lodging of any maid in England, keeping his room at an elegant hotel.

Maybe he was still there. Sleeping away the day, never planning to roll up his shirtsleeves and help with today's meals.

Yet if he didn't intend to return, why would he have come so far to see her? And bring her strawberries?

She couldn't fathom. But she also couldn't wait any longer. She had to leave now or risk missing the pick of today's offerings at the butcher, the greengrocer, and the fishmonger. Just as she was setting aside her cap and cramming her everyday hat onto her head, Jack entered the kitchen with a small parcel in hand.

"Morning, Mrs. Redfern," he said with a wink, and with entirely too much good cheer for a man who was going to peel vegetables all day.

"Good morning," she grumbled back, wishing for a cup of tea from the kettle she hadn't yet heated. These mornings when she went for supplies were always a scramble. "What's the parcel? You've been shopping at this hour?"

"No, I went shopping *before* this hour. You told me we'd have to rise early. Here, look what I got for you."

He handed over the little package, pulling loose the twine as he did. When Marianne took it in her hands, the paper fell open to reveal a palm-sized section of honeycomb. Sunlight-gold honey dewed the intricate little hexagons. Each was a reservoir for the sweet liquid, each itself of pleasant-scented wax.

The sight and smell of it tugged powerfully at her memory. When she brought the honeycomb to her nose to breathe in the scent, suddenly she was twenty years old again—back in Lincolnshire, wearing thick, long gloves and a hat with netting to protect her face. And she was laughing, telling the bees in her father's hives that Jack Grahame had asked her to marry him. This was an old tradition, really more of a superstition. One had to tell the bees of any weddings to come, or they'd grieve at being left out of the celebration and might stop making honey.

But that marriage never happened. Instead, Jack's father arranged his son's wedding with the well-dowered daughter of a wealthy merchant.

When the banns were called for Jack and Helena Wilcox, Marianne hadn't bothered to tell the bees. Let them continue on, happy in their ignorance.

They hadn't stopped making honey, as far as she knew, but she hadn't been around long enough to collect it. She'd thought she was protecting herself by leaving before the banns were called a second time. She *had* protected herself.

But she'd hurt herself too. There was so much she had missed by fleeing her home.

"Where did you get this honeycomb?" she asked.

Jack doffed his hat, looking pleased. "I persuaded a confectioner to open early."

"Why?"

"I wanted to bring you some, because I was remembering the bees your father used to keep."

So. He recalled those days too. "Why?"

Now he looked annoyed. "I don't know, Marianne. Maybe because seeing you reminds me of the way we grew up, helping the beekeeper collect honey and wax, and it was a nice memory, and I wanted to share it with you."

Yet all of that belonged firmly in the past. The Redfern land now belonged to the Grahames, sold by Marianne's mother upon being widowed five years before. Jack's father had been living then, and he'd snapped it up using the Wilcox money that had passed into his hands.

There was no room for Marianne and Jack in that memory anymore, certainly not together.

"That's not what I'm asking, really." She bit her lip, wishing for a taste of sweetness. "Why…any of this? You came to London. You brought me strawberries."

"And honeycomb," he pointed out.

"I don't understand why you're *here*, Jack. I have a good post, and you have your life in Lincolnshire. If you just wanted to share a memory, why didn't you send a letter?"

Seeming to think over his answer, he flipped his hat end over end. Fidget, fidget. "Because," he decided, "I haven't seen you for eight years, but for all the years before that, I saw you every day."

The kitchen clock chimed the hour, reminding her of time rushing past. "After eight years without seeing me, it seems as if you could go on in the same way."

"I probably could have, but I didn't want to." His gray eyes were merry. Why did he always look as if things were going his way? "Now that I'm here, maybe I'll begin to pine for you. Be a devoted suitor and shower you with gifts. Would you be interested?"

The fiend. Did he know that was all she'd once wanted?

Did she know what she wanted from him now?

With one fingertip, she touched the delicate comb—then, in a rush, she folded over the heavy brown paper and set the parcel down on the worktable. "Don't buy me any more presents."

"Why not?"

"Because it's not right."

He set his hat on the table beside the parcel, then stripped off his gloves. "You don't like them?"

"I don't know if I like them or not. It's too confusing."

His smile was crooked, not exactly happy. "I don't mind confusing you, Marianne. That's a step up from angering you, and isn't that where we started?"

"I don't know," she blurted. "You're confusing me."

He poked through the paper and touched the discarded honeycomb with a gentle forefinger. Then he folded the brown paper over it, packing it away. Done, Marianne thought. He'd listen, and he'd stop now.

Instead, he said, "Then I'll keep right on." Stepping closer, he cradled her face in his hands—and he kissed her.

Oh! She hadn't been kissed for so long. At first, the sensation startled her. Her mouth was meant for tasting recipes, for hectoring grocers, for explaining her work to assistants. It had been so long since she'd used it for anything else, for pure pleasure unconnected with work, that she was clumsy. The touch of his lips was too intimate; it was impossible to resist. She moved forward, crushing into Jack, and pressed her mouth against his. As if eager for her, his lips parted, taking her deeper.

She remembered this feeling now, this taste. The sweetness of a loved one face-to-face. The velvet touch of a tongue and the heat of lips. His strong fingers holding her face as if he couldn't bear for her to escape him again—

But she had. Had to. Did. Must.

She was at work, and anyone could happen in and *see* them, and—and she was a *cook* now, and she had meat and vegetables to buy.

Her thoughts in a tumble, she drew back, catching her heel on the hem of her work dress and staggering. Hands outstretched, palms facing him, she recovered her balance and asked again, "Why?"

Blinking as if dazed, he asked, "Why not?"

She set her hat straight. Drove a pin through the brim into her thick coil of hair. "That's the difference between us. I can't afford to ask why not."

He rubbed a hand over his chin, his mouth. "It's just a kiss, Marianne."

"Is it?" She swallowed.

Those gray eyes weren't merry now. "No. It wasn't just a kiss. But I thought if I said that, you might stop stumbling around and looking so worried and hurt."

"I'm not hurt," she said.

"And worried?"

She spoke slowly, as if reading out an unfamiliar recipe. "The only thing I'm worried about is missing all the choice grocery goods."

"Really? That's what's bothering you?" He lifted a brow.

"What else?" she said loftily, tying the strings of her bonnet, fighting the urge to lift her hand to her lips to see whether they felt as different without as they did within.

"If you say so, Mrs. Redfern." He popped his fashionable hat back atop his head, then pulled on the kid gloves entirely unsuited to a kitchenmaid's errands. "Lead on, and I'll serve you as you like."

He'd intended it in a teasing way, but he soon learned that Marianne took his offer of assistance all too literally. She'd given him an enormous basket to carry, and after visiting a dry-goods grocer, it groaned and clinked with jars and tins. The march from there to the greengrocer's seemed miles long as the basket dug into his arm and butted him in the leg.

Hitching it onto a different part of his forearm, he set his teeth. He'd have bruises all up and down his arms from the damned basket. Why had she had to get every spice in the world, and the bigger the container, the better?

"You've been picking heavy things on purpose," he grumbled to Marianne, blithely unburdened at his side.

Beneath the brim of her bonnet, her eyes squeezed with amusement. "Why, Jack, are you telling me that basket is too much for you?"

"No," he lied, pride stung. "Only, I don't understand why you couldn't have these things sent to the academy along with the other food."

"Because you're here to carry them. And what a fine kitchenmaid you are." Under straight dark brows, her eyes were large and full of humor.

"Ha," he said flatly, settling the heavy affair of wicker more firmly in the crook of his elbow.

Any landowner worth the name had been up with the animals at some time, had got his hands dirty in every field at one time or another. But dawn on Jack's rolling, quiet lands up north had left him wholly unprepared for an early morning in London's bustling food markets. Every street was a jostling wall of people, the cries of hawkers mixing with the *ding* of shop bells and the babble of customers and food sellers. The sun was pale in a spring-morning sky, but already Jack was hot, and he was gritty-eyed from little sleep and wondering how the devil Marianne could move through these crowds all the time.

"You really do this every day?"

"Not every day." She smiled. "Sometimes I make a list and send a footman. When I had an assistant and a proper kitchenmaid, I could send one of them."

"You imply that I'm not a proper kitchenmaid." He feigned distress. "So hurtful."

"But accurate. If you knew your ingredients, you'd never have suggested that huge sugarloaf."

"It's a large academy. We need a lot of sugar."

"Yes, but the larger loaves of sugar are from the later boilings. They don't cook or bake nearly so nicely as the first or second."

"Sugar...boils?" Surely she was speaking some sort of foreign language only cooks understood. "But it's solid."

She laughed. "Give me those two weeks, and you'll learn right enough how sugar boils. And gets made."

He eyed the basket into which several of the small, and apparently better, cone-shaped sugarloaves were nestled alongside expensive vanilla pods, fragrant cinnamon, and God only knew what else. "Fine, as long as I don't have to shop with this cursed basket all the time."

"Just this once, to give you the experience." She slipped a hand onto his unladen arm. "Ah, here's the greengrocer. Isn't this nice? Getting out of the kitchen and into the city? Really, though it throws the day into a flurry, I enjoy the shopping. Picking out all the best for the young ladies and the teachers, keeping them fed and happy with the food I make. It's part of their learning. Part of helping them become…whatever they're going to become."

He eyed her with some surprise. "What sort of academy is this, that you feed them so well and care so much?"

She looked embarrassed then, turning her gaze to the lettuces and becoming brisk. "Well. Everyone needs to eat, and it's my job to feed them. Good morning, Mr. Haviland!" She greeted the greengrocer, a stocky, beetle-browed man with a pleasant smile and the cutthroat negotiating ability of a pirate. Jack had encountered this fellow the day before when he'd bought strawberries, little knowing he'd soon be back for more produce as an employee of the academy.

Informally. Voluntarily.

And, despite his present physical discomforts, not at all unhappily.

Marianne was engaging in a spirited and fluent battle of prices with Haviland, finally shaking her head. "No, the lettuce is simply too dear. We'll make do with—what could I cook?" She ticked on her fingers, thinking. "I'll have the cabbages."

Ugh. Cabbages. No. "Allow me to make up the difference, Marianne," Jack offered. "Look—I know this man. I bought strawberries from him yesterday." Haviland was beaming, remembering, probably, what an easy mark Jack had been. He couldn't deny it. He'd got used to having money and to using it to save trouble.

Marianne looked at Jack repressively.

Oh. His informality. "Mrs. Redfern," he corrected. "Ma'am."

Again, she shook her head. "No, don't buy the lettuce at that price. It's not that I can't spend more of Mrs. Brodie's money if I wish. The headmistress allows me free rein. But if I spend too much, I don't enjoy working with the ingredients. If the cost is too dear, all the joy is gone."

She turned back to the greengrocer, her cheeks pink with the pleasure of arguing. And Jack, holding her basket, reeled on his feet.

Not because of lettuce, or even cabbage. But because she was right: When the cost was too dear, there was no way to find joy. He and Helena had sold themselves, she for status and he for money. He'd loved someone else, and she had too.

The cost had been too dear. And when Lincolnshire had seen loss upon loss—Marianne's father, the Redfern lands, Helena, his own father—Jack stopped counting the months to the end of mourning and began instead counting the months until he could get away. To Marianne, with whom he'd last been happy in that golden, glowing, honeycomb way.

"Forget the lettuce," she concluded with a sniff. "Mr. Haviland, I'll take the cabbages instead. Jack, by the time I'm done with them, you'll swear they were tender spring greens."

She tapped her chin with a fingertip. "How many do you suppose we could fit into that basket? I'll need twenty-three for the academy meal, and for the servants' dinner...hmm."

"Wait. You make a whole separate dinner for the servants?"

Her brows drew together. "Of course I do. You don't think the kitchenmaids dine on roasted lambs and new peas with shallots, do you?"

He resettled the basket, growing heavy again on his arm. "I rather hoped this kitchenmaid would."

She elbowed him, grinning. "The meal will be as good as you help me make it. We'll have colcannon, and you see if Mrs. Lavery doesn't come into the kitchens for a serving of it."

"Mrs. Lavery?" Jack didn't recognize the name as one of the servants he'd met the day before.

"She's the—" Biting her lip, she shot a glance at the greengrocer. "The art teacher, among other things. Family's from Ireland. She made sure I've got the recipe just right."

To the order of cabbages, she added onions as well, selecting them carefully as a wealthy lady might pick over the stones at Rundell and Bridge. After arranging to have the vegetables delivered to the academy, she rejected the leeks the greengrocer offered. "Good in colcannon, but not if they look dry as that. Nice try, Mr. Haviland."

The man threw up his hands in seeming dismay, then bade a farewell so cheerful that it was clear he'd enjoyed the dickering as much as Marianne had. As they left the stands of fruit and vegetables, Jack was simply relieved not to have dozens of cabbages piled onto the clinking weight of the exotic ingredients in the basket.

"We'll go to the butcher's next," Marianne said, pushing back into the thick of the crowd of shoppers. "And find a bit of bacon to go into the servants' dinner, plus joints of beef for the young ladies."

"One moment," Jack said. "I've got to switch arms, since you're using me instead of a farm wagon." He shifted the basket, drawing it from his aching left forearm to the right and immediately felt pinioned.

It was then that he noticed the dip. If it had been subtle, he probably wouldn't have, but this was a jostle against his side, a hand in his coat.

He struggled to turn, fighting the press of several people moving past him at once. Who had done it? A boy? No, a grown man! That wiry balding fellow, just there. Jack saw the purse just before someone moved between them, blocking both his sight and path to the man.

"Stop! Thief!" Jack thrust the huge basket into Marianne's arms, then gave chase. "Stop that bald man!" he called. "Thief!" Damn these crowds! Why was everyone in his way? Hadn't they heard him? Seen the man running away with his purse?

Shoving and pushing, he finally got close enough to dive for his quarry. With a leap and a curse, he caught the man about the shoulders and tackled him down.

"Lemme go! I didn't do anything!" The wiry man struggled, caught Jack in the bruised forearm, and slipped from his grasp as Jack hissed in pain.

A neat booted foot stuck out—to trip the man, Jack thought with a flicker of hope, but no, it caught another fellow and sent him sprawling. The balding man darted away, looking over his shoulder furtively, as Jack turned to lambaste his would-be helper.

It was no well-meaning stranger who regarded him with grave green eyes.

"Marianne!" How had she run after him so quickly? He shook that off. "That's not the thief!" The man she had tripped was larger and quite prosperous looking. Already, he was heaving himself upright, indignant and blustering.

Marianne moved closer to the man, saying something Jack couldn't hear, and held out her hand. In a flash, it all changed. The proper gentleman's face contorted, and he caught her about the throat and pulled her against his body with an arm like a vise. Jack's heart, already hammering from the chase, skipped and stuttered. "No!" He lunged forward, ready to attack.

Then Marianne sank in a faint, poor thing, her knees buckling. Jack twisted to catch her—but no, she wasn't collapsing as he'd thought. She'd got the man to loosen his hold, and she bent abruptly at the waist, flipping the much larger man over her body.

Jack could only gape as the large man was somersaulted over Marianne, landing flat on his back on the pavement. With a single stride, Marianne went to the groaning man's side and planted her foot gently on his throat.

"Stay down," she said coolly, "and don't cause any more mischief. And give my kitchenmaid back what your accomplice stole from him."

"Accomplice...?" Jack had no idea what was going on. How had Marianne flung a grown man over her head like that? And where was the man who had stolen Jack's money?

A constable arrived on the scene and took charge of the prone man from Marianne. A search of his pockets revealed not only Jack's purse, but several others—more than enough to haul him off, despite his protests that he'd never stolen a thing.

"He'll be giving up his accomplice within five minutes." Marianne dusted her hands on her skirts, then straightened her hat. All perfectly untroubled, seeming heedless of the curious crowd about. "All right, then, Jack? I have to go back and get my basket from Mr. Haviland. We'd best count all the jars to make sure he hasn't helped himself."

"How..." Jack shook his head. "I don't understand. How did you know who had my purse? That wasn't the man who stole it."

"The dip was so clumsy. He couldn't expect to get away with it unless he handed off the goods to someone else, and I saw him do it. If you'd caught the first fellow, he wouldn't have so much as a stolen farthing on him." Jack must have been staring, for she added, "It's not so uncommon a scheme here in London. Especially on a busy street."

Jack kept a hand to his purse—impressed, intrigued, and not a little intimidated. "And you deal with this every day." As they retraced their steps to the greengrocer's, he asked the more pressing question. "*Where* did you learn to flip a grown man over your head?"

"Well, it wasn't over my head. But I learned it from Miss Carpenter. She teaches geometry and mathematics at the academy."

He remembered her pause when she was describing the job of Mrs. Lavery, who apparently liked eating colcannon. "She teaches something else too, I'll warrant."

"Oh—perhaps. You did all right for someone who hasn't had her instruction. You almost had that first fellow."

Retrieving the basket from the bemused Mr. Haviland, Jack resettled it on his arm. For the second time, he asked, "What sort of academy *is* this?"

Marianne grinned at him. "Maybe this evening, you'd like to find out.

## Chapter Three

Jack had looked forward to one of Miss Carpenter's lessons that evening. It would be interesting, he thought, to learn her methods for flipping grown humans over one's head.

Interesting? That was putting the matter mildly.

Within three minutes of entering the ballroom for the lesson, Jack had seen enough to realize Marianne had let that thief's accomplice off easy by only tossing him to the pavement.

Within another two minutes, Jack had been volunteered—though not precisely voluntarily—to play the part of an attacker toward Marianne, and he himself had been heaved through the air and onto a sawdust-stuffed mat that wasn't nearly thick enough.

"One can use the human body as a l-lever to move much larger masses," explained Miss Carpenter, a square-shouldered, freckled young woman with red-blond hair and a deceptively sweet face. "A-as the Greek scientist Archimedes is thought to have said,

'Give me a lever long enough and a place to stand and I can move the earth.' But in Greek, of course."

She regarded Jack, still prone on the floor, with approval. "G-good, Mr. G-grahame. You l-landed just r-right." Her stammer came and went, present when addressing Jack but almost absent when speaking to the others in the room, whom she clearly knew well.

Besides Jack and Marianne, six others were present for the lesson. Jack recognized one as the art teacher, Mrs. Lavery, who'd inspired the colcannon the servants had enjoyed for their evening meal. The teacher of history and geography was there too, a pretty widow named Mrs. Chalmers who had light brown skin and alarmingly intelligent eyes.

Also present were two students who were almost grown and preparing to become teachers themselves and a pair of footmen who looked visibly relieved that Jack had joined the group tonight. Miss Carpenter had introduced them as her assistants. Jack guessed they usually played the part of attackers being slammed to earth, or otherwise having the large masses of their human bodies used as levers against their own safety.

Jack groaned and stood, rubbing his shoulder. "It didn't *feel* like I landed well. Mrs. Redfern heaved me like a sack of cabbages."

Marianne beamed at him.

"You w-weren't hurt," said Miss Carpenter. "N-not r-really. Kn-knowing how to fall is as important as kn-knowing how to get away."

"Or attack," he grumbled. Yet he felt lifted by the response, as if he'd somersaulted over Marianne's head with skill rather than landing by ungraceful chance.

Miss Carpenter then broke the group into pairs to practice holds and escapes, settling one of the footmen with each of the students and the two other teachers with each other. As this left Jack with Marianne, he stood by her side and murmured in her ear, "Turnabout is fair play. I'll have you on your back in a minute."

She choked, covering a laugh. "Presumptuous, aren't you?"

Jack realized how his words had sounded. "Hm. More like loose-tongued. No, that's not any better, is it? You're still laughing."

She pressed a hand to her mouth and nodded.

He folded his arms, but completely failed at sternness. "Fine, then. Laugh. I'm a man with manly urges, and I'm not ashamed of it."

After he'd kissed her earlier, he'd thought about it all day, since chopping cabbage didn't prevent a man's mind from roaming. She'd liked the kiss; she'd deepened the kiss. And then her clever, organized mind had cleared its throat and interrupted them, and she'd been all business again.

But throughout the day, he'd caught her looking at him. Confused, as she'd said, and sometimes biting her lip. Remembering the kiss, or the taste of strawberries, or the honeycomb he'd found carefully wrapped and hidden behind the new sugarloaves in the pantry.

Maybe he wasn't the only one with urges.

Marianne pivoted to face him, a foot of space between them on the mat. "Your manly urges didn't keep you from being thrown like a—how did you put it? A sack of cabbages?"

All right, maybe he *was* the only one with urges. "Do your worst, Cook. I've handled more cabbages today than you, and I'm not a bit afraid."

"You were going to have me on my back, I think you said. Would you like to try it?"

Through the wide windows, the sky still held the final shreds of daylight, while branches of candles kept their corner of the ballroom glowing warm and welcoming. Oh, she looked saucy, her eyes shining and hair glinting auburn in the candlelight. She still wore her faded work dress from the day, but her hair was plaited now and pinned into a coronet about her head. It looked playful yet regal, and if she didn't stop laughing, he just might pluck out those pins and give reality to his promise.

"I'll not only try it," he said, "I'll make it happen."

He scrutinized the other pairs for clues, soon understanding why the footmen were willing to allow themselves to be flung about. Miss Carpenter was settling the hands of one of the students on a footman's wrist, instructing the young woman to tug the man's arm forward. As the student obliged, putting pressure on the man's elbow joint, his expression looked anything but discomfited. It was half an embrace, the lucky fellow.

As Miss Carpenter moved along to the next pair, demonstrating the lunge and tug, Marianne faced Jack.

"You're watching what they do? Let's give a different move a try. Come at me as if you'd like to kick me in the midsection."

Jack regarded her doubtfully. "I like your midsection. I don't want to kick it."

"If I've learned my lesson from Miss Carpenter, you won't even come close." She looked about. "Here, we'd better stand over one of the mats."

Dubious still, Jack stepped back. Then he strode forward, one great step and another, and turned on the ball of his foot to kick out sideways toward Marianne.

Though he'd expected some skullduggery, he hadn't foreseen her quick movement. She seized him about the leg in a tight embrace. Thus pinned—though not unhappily—he struggled to keep his balance. "You've made your point," he said. "You're strong and clever. Now let go. I look like a ballerina."

Over the line of his leg, her frank eyes met his. "I'm sorry about this," she said. A second later, a kick to his standing foot knocked that leg out from under him, sending him to the mat flat on his face.

Only then did she let go of his leg. As he groaned, stunned, she crouched next to him. "All right?"

"You're a terrible human being."

"I *did* apologize," she pointed out. "But wasn't it clever? You could use the same tricks if anyone ever attacks you."

"No one would ever attack me in Lincolnshire. And the only person who attacks me in London is you." Settling his hands under himself, he pushed up into a plank, then slid his feet beneath him and stood.

Miss Carpenter stopped beside them then. "Another good f-fall, Mr. Grahame." She looked to Marianne. "A-are you comfortable trying the throat grab?"

"Throat grab?" Jack's brows shot up. "No. I'm not comfortable trying the throat grab. No one grabs my throat."

"It works the other way. With you grabbing me." Marianne's cheeks went pink. "Jack, take hold of me as if you want to throttle me."

With a knowing smile—just what did she think she knew?—Miss Carpenter moved off to work with another pair. And Jack faced Marianne, less than an arm's length away.

He stepped closer. "You said 'as if I want to throttle you.' Taking it for granted that I don't, after what you've put me through?"

"You said you wanted to see what sort of academy this is." Her eyes were fathomless, lovely. "And I've hurt you only today, and only your pride."

Which meant, he supposed, that he had hurt her far more over the years. It must have seemed to her, gone from Lincolnshire and knowing his life only through vague rumor, that he'd got everything he wanted and moved along from her.

Secondhand news never got the details right. Sometimes he hadn't known what to make of his own life, and he was the one steeped in it.

He stepped forward and set one hand to each side of her neck, cradling it in a gentle collar. Her skin was smooth and warm; he stroked it with the pad of his thumb, up and down, until her head tipped to one side to allow him greater range of motion.

"I'm throttling you," he said quietly. "What do I do now?"

She blinked slowly. "Ah...now I take hold of you." She grabbed his arms above the elbows and pulled him tightly against her body.

"Dear me," Jack said thickly. "Which of us is attacking which?"

"Now...now we lie on the floor." She was still blushing.

"You mean I get you on your back." He knew he was smirking.

"I mean I pull you to the floor." She leaned backward, taking them down in a swift tangle of limbs.

For once, it didn't hurt to fall—or maybe the aches merely faded in the face of arousal. His hands were still on her neck, and he slid them to her collarbone, to the lovely sliver of uncovered skin above the bodice of her dress. She clutched him about the arms, preventing him from freeing himself—as if he'd be fool enough to want to when he lay over her like a lover in bed. Just a fraction, he dipped his head, and when her lids fluttered shut and lips parted, he decided fighting was his new favorite subject.

Another inch, and he'd claim her mouth, and then he would—

"No, n-no. That's not it at all, Mr. Grahame. Mrs. Redfern. James, come here."

Jack's head snapped up. Marianne's eyes snapped open. With what probably seemed like suspicious speed, they untangled themselves and scooted away from each other on the mat.

Miss Carpenter was the one who had spoken. Reluctantly, one of the footmen shuffled away from his pliant, smiling partner and toward the instructor.

Once Jack and Marianne moved aside, this pair took up places on the mat. What followed was the throat grab and arm grasp, a sudden yank back, and some sort of collapsing somersault on the part of the teacher, and the unfortunate flip of James, heels over head, to land on his back.

The young teacher bounced to her feet, then extended a hand to her partner and heaved him upright. "See the difference? Y-you need to fold at the w-waist, Mrs. Redfern, and place a foot at his m-middle. Make a spring of your body to propel him into the air."

"Don't listen to her. Don't fold at the waist," Jack murmured into Marianne's ear as they sat at the edge of the mat. "Don't place a foot in his middle and propel him into the air. Let him lie on top of you instead."

She snorted. "That wouldn't be much of a defense, would it?"

"And why would you defend against me?"

"Many reasons," she said with a sigh.

That didn't sound like a bad thing, but he stood and offered Marianne a hand to help her up. Instead of rising to her feet, she took hold of his hand, then his arm at the elbow, and pulled him down again. One of her feet came up to catch his belly, not as a kick but as balance, and instead of his body flipping over hers, they again collapsed in a heap.

"N-not quite how I meant it," said Miss Carpenter.

But if their instructor said anything else, Jack didn't notice as he looked into Marianne's face. He noticed only the swiftness of Marianne's breathing, the wicked curl of her lips. The softness of her breasts beneath his chest and the length of her limbs entangled with his.

And she thought *she* had to defend against *him.*

"Had we best be done with today's lesson?" he asked, addressing his words not to Miss Carpenter, but to the lovely woman who had tugged his body against hers.

"I think we had, yes," Marianne replied, a hitch in her voice.

That was that. And a wise thing, too. Regretfully, slowly, Jack levered himself up from their prone position and helped Marianne upright. After he thanked Miss Carpenter for her instruction and bade good night to the others, he and Marianne exited the ballroom. "I'd best be off to my hotel, so I can be ready to work at first light."

She didn't quite look at him. "Not yet. There is more work I need of you here. Tonight."

"Truly? There cannot be a vegetable in London left unchopped."

Still, she didn't look at him, and the candles in the corridor sconces left her face in shadow. "It's not chopping vegetables I have in mind."

Oh. *Oh.* He thought he understood her meaning, but decided to toy with her a bit. "Indeed? Could you be more specific?"

"Come on, Jack," she said with some impatience. "I know you liked lying on top of me. I—could tell."

"Of course I liked lying on top of you. Remember? Manly urges."

"Are you still having them? The manly urges?"

She tipped her face to look up at him, and he couldn't be flippant anymore. Not with her eyes on him, so beautifully familiar in shape, so vulnerable and seeking. They'd grown apart; she was offering them a chance to be together again.

Even if he hadn't had manly urges—which, by God, he did—he'd be a fool to say no.

"For you?" he replied, smoothing back a wisp of her dark hair, loving the feel of her, *real*, here. "Always. Forever."

She laced her fingers with his, then, and pulled him through quiet corridors and through the door that separated the main part of the academy from the servants' quarters below. They descended the narrow steps to the basement kitchens, silent under the weight of wanting that filled the space between them. Every stride was too short to cover the distance remaining; every breath was too long to wait to touch her more.

When they reached the kitchens, still and empty for the night, Jack was following her blindly, his eyes wide against the pressing darkness. His footsteps rang heavily on the flagstone floor, obvious and blundering. Marianne guided him through the warren of small rooms, through a doorway, then closed it behind her. She struck a flint and tinder, then lit a lamp to reveal a tiny chamber beside the butler's pantry.

"What room is this?" Jack asked, eyeing the simple bed, the screen, the washstand on which Marianne had replaced the lamp.

"It's mine," Marianne replied. "I've this chamber, and the housekeeper and butler have a great large room at the other end of the basement. The other servants are up in the attics."

"This is where you live?" Curious, Jack studied the space. There was nothing to show this room belonged to Marianne, or indeed to any particular person. Besides the clothes hanging on hooks behind the screen, it might have been a bare chamber left unused.

"No. The kitchen is where I live. This is where I sleep." She reached her hands out to him. "And where we can…"

"Ah. You want me to slake my manly urges with you," he said lightly, though the sight of the room troubled him. She was a gentleman's daughter, and she lived with almost nothing. Was she at the edge of poverty? What would happen to her if she couldn't work anymore?

Questions he'd never thought to ask until he'd realized his family had no more money. Questions he felt compelled to resolve now that his finances were secure.

"Come with me to my hotel room," he offered. "There's a feather bed, with more than enough room for you to stay the night, and—"

"Jack. No." She lifted a hand, laid it gently over his lips. "This is where I live. It's where I belong now." She gestured broadly, encompassing the servants' quarters as a whole. "If you want to be with me, be with me here."

He pressed a kiss to her hand, then pulled it from his face. Taking her into his arms, he replied, "I want to be with you."

So he was. And after much undressing, and kissing, and caresses and laughter and a pleasure almost shattering, he had to admit that there was nothing at all wrong with a narrow bed in a plain room, as long as one shared it with the right person.

In a tangle of limbs, they fell asleep.

## Chapter Four

Marianne awoke when the lamp guttered out, her eyes snapping open in the darkness. Without lamplight, it was always dark in this windowless room, but she'd a good internal clock, and she knew it wasn't yet time to awake for the day.

Who was she fooling? Not only the sudden fall of darkness had awoken her. The press of Jack's warm, lean body against hers—almost nudging her off the edge of the bed—had unsettled her sleep too. The sensitive space between her legs, the tingle of her skin where he'd touched it—these things had pervaded her dreams and made her wakeful, wistful.

"Marianne," he said quietly, and his arm came around her to settle beneath her bare breasts.

"The lamp went out," she whispered. "It woke me, but I'll drift off again."

"I want to tell you some things," he replied, "and it'll be easier in the dark."

She wiggled under his arm, apprehensive. "Bad things?"

"No. Just…old things. Honest things."

"All right. I can listen to old and honest things." She rolled toward him on the bed. Though she couldn't see his face, she knew it to be close. His arm cradled her, tugged her against his body so her nipples brushed his chest.

"When I was twenty-one, twenty-two…before you went away," he began, "I had nothing to offer but the circumstances of my birth. My maleness. Connected to that were the responsibilities of my father's land, the tenants my grandfather and his father had placed there, and all the generations of tradition before that."

"I always thought you had more to offer than that." She rocked her torso, liking the feeling of his chest hair against her breasts.

He didn't seem to notice; he must have been deep in thought indeed. "My father arranged the marriage with Helena Wilcox so I could safeguard them all. I felt cheap for doing it, yet it helped so many. Two of my sisters have married well, and all three of them found love. I have nieces and nephews. The tenants' cottages are in good repair, the land is healthy, and the crops have been more than fair."

If he'd sounded proud, she would have thought him boasting. But he didn't sound happy at all. "Why are you telling me all this?" she asked. "I don't care. That is—I do. I'm glad for those people. But it's no part of my life, and I never thought it would be."

"Exactly." His breath tickled her ear, making a wisp of hair dance. "You agreed to marry me without thinking of what it would mean in the years ahead. You agreed only because you liked me."

"I loved you," she said faintly. Not knowing whether she ought to speak the phrase in the past tense, or the present.

"My father didn't understand that. He didn't marry for love. Not that he was a bad man; he was a responsible landowner and respectful husband and dutiful father. But—it didn't *matter* to him that I loved you. Not compared to making a marriage that would help our family in the present and future."

"This might be too honest for me." Marianne pushed against his chest, putting space between them. "I don't want to hear that I weighed too little against your father's wishes. I already *know* that. I lived it."

He trailed his fingers lightly over her shoulder, her ribs, letting his hand rest at her waist. "Then I haven't explained it well. I could have turned my back on him for you, and had it only been a matter of his will, I would have. But it was tenants. Livelihoods. The future. Hungry bellies and hopeful eyes.

"If it were only up to me," he added, "the scale would never balance against you. Not then, not now, not ever."

His hand on her waist was a weight, making it hard for her to draw breath. "But it's not only up to you."

"Not then, not now, not ever." His tone was quiet. "But the hope's now in my eyes, and the scale is yours to balance, Marianne. I've seen everyone else taken care of but you. And me."

"I don't expect or want you to take care of me." After his low tone, she sounded harsh.

He hesitated. "I know you don't need it." Then his hand stroked Marianne's side again. Quick trailing fingertips, halting movements. "My marriage wasn't really anything of the sort. Helena—she loved my sister Viola. Not me. And Viola loved her in return."

This was unexpected news. "Your wife...loved your sister?" Marianne had always assumed Helena Wilcox, pretty and rich and kind, had given her heart to Jack. Who wouldn't? And of course, living as man and wife, he would have come to love her in return.

"Her love for Viola is why Helena agreed to marry me." His hand went still, the palm flat and heated on her side. "I thought you might suspect, when after Helena's death, you addressed letters of condolence to my mother and sister."

"I did that to show how proper I was. That as a spinster, I wouldn't write to a man." Her thoughts were in a jumble, as if she were trying to sort out parts of two different recipes and combine them into one. But how did this fit—? And did that mean—?

"You were so proper that I completely misunderstood," Jack said dryly.

"That's half the purpose of manners."

"Maybe so." Jack chuckled. "We had separate chambers, Helena and I, from the moment of the wedding. Her chamber was…much closer to my sister's than it was to mine. Both women were happier that way."

"Oh," was all Marianne could say. There had been a great deal to balance against the possibility of her marriage to Jack. Even more than she'd realized.

"When Helena died," Jack said, "Viola grieved her as a spouse. I grieved the loss of a friend who had done me a great kindness."

"Bringing all that money to your marriage," Marianne said. Money, money, money. She usually wanted to punch down dough when she thought of it. Now she didn't know *what* she wanted.

"Yes," he said simply. "And along with her, I grieved the end of my marriage. Though it was in name only, I'd changed my whole life for it. What was I to do now?"

She rested a hand on his face, wanting to feel each nuance of movement, of expression. "You'd money enough to do whatever you wanted."

"So I did." He smiled, cheek and lips moving under her touch. "So I did."

She half expected him to say he'd come tearing after her at once, though she knew it wasn't true. He'd been widowed for a proper two years now. "What did you do with all the time since?" she finally asked.

"Amidst the conventions of mourning, I made myself the sort of man I'd always wanted to be. I learned languages. I studied drainage to improve my land. I made my body strong with fencing and running. I read history and mathematics. I visited the ailing and needy. I went to church every week. It was only then I realized that, worthy though my pursuits were, I was only filling time. I wasn't happy myself. I felt nothing but duty and the savorless pleasure of obligations fulfilled. I missed feeling more."

"Oh." Should she say more? She didn't know what it should be, yet there was clearly more to say.

"That's when I came here to see you."

"Oh," she said again, softened. She traced the shape of his features, his jaw, the line of his ear. There was much she needed to learn about him, and to relearn.

"I can speak to you in Italian or French or German, or even Latin," he said dryly. "I can check the drainage around the house or convert your recipes into large quantities and take beef tea to a sick student."

She laughed. "You forgot to say anything about church or fencing." She laced her fingers into the short silk of his hair. "It's all still *things*, Jack. And," she couldn't resist adding, "what I most need now is a man who can chop four dozen cabbages without nicking his thumb."

"Ah, well. You can't blame me for trying to impress you, can you? Though I studied all the wrong things for that. Should have practiced with a knife and a basket of vegetables every once in a while."

"You impress me more when you don't try." She was glad now for the darkness, not wanting him to see the blush that heated her cheeks.

He turned his head, pressing his face into her palm, then rested on the pillow again. "You impress me. The end. When I saw you, you looked different, but I knew you at once."

"How am I different?"

"You are…" He trailed off, evidently thinking over his response. Wise man. "More. More grown-up, more beautiful, more strong and determined."

Within, she melted. She was all syrups and honeys and glazes, sweet and pliant. She couldn't bring a bit of sauce to her tongue as she asked quietly, "And did you feel something?"

"Yes. I felt," he said simply.

They lay together in silence for a half-dozen heartbeats. A dozen, then another. It would never be enough heartbeats, and anything she said would not be enough either.

"I don't worry about money anymore." Jack's hand slid from her side, trailed up, covered her heart. "What I worry about now is never being as happy as Helena was with my sister."

"Do you expect me to make you happy?"

"I rather hoped we could make each other happy. We did once."

They had, when they'd thought they had forever. But what did they have now? Another hour? A night? A fortnight, or however long he chose to stay in London?

She didn't want to ask; she didn't want the answer. So she asked something else instead. "Then you were never…you know. With Helena? Like this?"

"I never was," Jack confirmed. "Since you."

She drew his hand from her heart to cover her breast. "Then we'd better do it again," she said. Before morning came and washed away the intimacy of the night.

The first time he'd come into her, she'd given him her body. This second time, she let herself fall in love again. He was everywhere: her body, her mind, her heart. And though he moved atop her, with her, she felt lighter.

In the morning he was still there. He'd kept her in his arms throughout the night.

He had chosen her; he had stayed with her.

And so she forgave him at last.

## *Chapter Five*

For the next several days, Marianne put Jack to work in earnest as a kitchenmaid, helping Sally with tasks for the day's meals while Marianne worked ahead for the Donor Dinner. The whole academy staff thought of it in capital letters now, this looming feast for wealthy patrons that included an exhibition of student talents. There was little over a week to go and so much to prepare and plan.

The orders were placed for peas and mushrooms on the day of the dinner; the peas would be made into a soup, the mushrooms into a fricassee with meat of crab. Mushrooms would also serve as the side to a dish of salmon, served whole save for the head. The fishmonger was on alert, as was the dairymaid who provided cream and butter. Two days ahead, fresh-killed pheasant would be hung and singed, and the hares were already hanging in the meat safe, all the better for a bit of aging before they were jugged in wine. Oh! The wines… Marianne would have to ask Hobbes to decide the wines for each course and remove. The old butler had enough knowledge to fill a vineyard, as well as the poker-stiff bearing that impressed the beau monde even more than being served the proper wine at the proper time.

So little could be done ahead compared to what must be done the day before or day of. But the more Marianne planned, the easier the day's tasks would be. And the more she planned, the less she felt she'd be caught unawares; the less she worried about being left, startled, inadequate.

Of being unable to balance the scales. Of not being the right choice for the task.

If Jack knew she still worried about that, he didn't let on. He was cheerful with every day's work, as if he'd never wanted to be anywhere else, and never would, but this hot and hectic kitchen. From his seat at the end of the worktable, he peeled new carrots and trimmed asparagus, chopped new potatoes and grated the woody last of the year's parsnips. He listened as Marianne instructed Sally about the day's recipes: which seasonings work together, how to use less-than-perfect ingredients—such as those woody parsnips, which had come cheap and could be saved by boiling them, then frying them into crispy thin cakes.

"A cook has to improvise and substitute all the time," Marianne told Sally, remembering the apricot tarts of the day Jack had arrived—not only an improvised recipe, but an improvised kitchenmaid. "Sometimes it works out far better than the original plan."

She looked over at the end of the table. As if feeling her gaze, Jack looked up and winked, then returned to peeling and chopping onions. His short-cropped hair was uncovered, and though he'd taken off his coat, he was still unsuitably fine for kitchen tasks. But he rolled up his shirtsleeves with the confidence of a man who knew his arms looked well—and that he could simply buy other clothing if these were stained or damaged.

Marianne looked ruefully at her work dress, faded from blue to gray. Cut loose and comfortable, the fabric worn soft and thin from many washings. It was just right for what she had to do, yet it felt like not enough. And that feeling came from within herself, she knew, so she tried to quash it. To Jack, she was enough. He had come here; he had told her so; he had taken her in his arms. Several nights now, he'd come to her, though after the first, he had left after their lovemaking to return to his hotel. He couldn't be seen in the same clothing for days on end, he'd pointed out, which was sensible.

She knew that, yet she ached when he left her. She ached a bit now, looking at him across the room. Still not quite believing that he was content to clean vegetables all day just to be near her, and not able to cease wondering, *For how long?*

Somehow, working with onions never made him teary or sniffling; he looked as if he were tackling another of those accomplishments with which he'd filled his life before coming to London. Learn to fence. Master another language. Don an apron and become indispensable as kitchenmaid in a rather exceptional academy.

Don anything or strip off everything and become indispensable to Marianne. Full stop.

She cleared her throat, then turned back to Sally. "Another issue to consider: You might not always cook at the academy. Here, we feed a huge number, but we do it as we see fit. In an elegant household, the master or mistress could give you a menu, no matter how unreasonable, and you have to make it happen. If the mistress asks for parsnips in July, how can you make her happy with both you and the food you serve?"

Sally groaned. "As if parsnips aren't bad enough in May. Whatever was left in July would be all string and rot."

"So use a little—a very little—of what you can find, to obey your mistress. And make up the bulk of the recipe with…?" Marianne prompted, even as her mind whirled to answer the question. It would be a pleasant challenge. Parsley root was sometimes available in summer and would have a similar appearance. With a bit of treacle, it would work, maybe, though the root's flavor would be strong. Or a combination of—

"Apple and potato," Sally decided. "To get the creaminess and sweetness. If the lady wanted them in a mash. If she wanted them buttered and whole, I might as well resign my post."

Marianne laughed. "Very good! Not the plan to resign, but the alternative to parsnips. That would do quite well. You've come far, Sally—even if you are much too kind to the kitchenmaid."

Both Jack and Sally chuckled, then returned to their work. Sally was arranging sliced potatoes in an attractive pattern in the bottom of a giant pan, to then be covered with sliced onion from Jack. More potatoes, then a sauce Marianne would whisk together of egg and milk and butter and cheddar, and the lot would bake for the academy dinner along with the loins of pork already roasting.

As the other two worked, Marianne spread the plan of the table for the Donor Dinner before her. It grew in size and elegance each year, a testimony to the success of the academy. Now she would need to feed dozens of the elite, wanting only the best. Two courses, the first with a remove for soup, and a dessert. Each course must be arranged in a particular way, with center and side dishes in a harmony for appearance and taste…

She sketched an arrangement lightly with a pencil, considered, and added a few notes to her plan.

Then Jack started humming.

"Stop humming," Marianne said without looking up. "Just chop."

"It's too quiet."

Now she did look up, a protest on her lips. Too *quiet*? With the servants talking in their dining hall? With Evans rattling the coal scuttle? With Sally sliding metal pans over the table and pots rattling on their shelves when someone walked by?

She remembered this about him, how he liked always to be at the center of attention. Not to draw it to himself, but to soak in it.

"Fine," she said. "Talk if you must. But no humming."

"'Scuse me, mum, but I'll get the cheese and butter for the sauce," Sally said. "We'll be needing it soon."

The sauce. Today's meal. Right. Marianne tossed down the pencil and rubbed at her temples, drawing herself back to today's plans. "Cheese and butter," she said. "Thank you. Milk too, and fresh eggs, and the flour." Sometimes a sauce needed thickening, and adding flour was one of the simplest ways to correct the texture.

Sally bustled off, and Jack spoke up. "I'd rather listen than talk, if you're in the mood."

Marianne's eyes popped open. "Words every woman longs to hear, unless she's got a meal to prepare."

"You don't have anything to do until Sally gets back." Those merry gray eyes, those wicked gray eyes.

"All right, Mr. Grahame." She stressed the surname, then rested her weight on the corner of the table at his side. "For perhaps four minutes, I am at my leisure."

He popped to his feet, pressed a quick kiss to her lips, then sat again and resumed peeling the papery skin off an onion. All before she had even finished gasping her surprise.

"Why did you never come back to Lincolnshire?" he asked.

She picked up an onion skin, folding and crumpling it between her fingertips. "Too proud," she admitted. "Unless I could return in triumph, I planned never to go back at all."

He nodded at the scattered makings on the worktable—the plan for the Donor Dinner, the pan of sliced potatoes. "Look at what you bring together every day. Isn't that a triumph?"

She smiled. "That's not a…" Then she paused. "It is, isn't it? It's not the sort of triumph I was thinking of, but yes. It's a triumph."

Jack sliced a bad spot out of an onion. "You were thinking of the sort of triumph one reads about in novels, weren't you? With a husband who adores you and gems all over?"

"Right," she agreed. Though hadn't she always liked strawberries more than gems? "Right," she reassured herself. Because if she'd had enough all this time, and she could have gone home to her remaining family whenever she missed them…

She blinked, her eyes teary. "Onions are getting to me." As she moved away from Jack, she added, "My life is in London."

Jack shrugged. "Sure it is, part of it."

"All of it," she said firmly, though she felt as wobbly as an underdone blancmange.

"You know, when your father died and your mother sold the Redfern lands to my father, all that money went to set up an income for your mother and dowries for her daughters."

"I know." Marianne's two younger sisters were three and six years her junior. They had both married as they wished, thanks to the freedom of money. Money, money, money.

She was still holding the onion skin. She crumpled it and threw it to the floor.

"All *three* daughters," Jack said. "Not only your sisters."

"I know," she said again, though she'd hardly thought of it since receiving the news five years before. "But I can't make use of a dowry."

He nodded as if this made perfect sense, to turn away from thousands of pounds—though he'd never done it himself. "Your mother has it now. She lives in the dower house on my property with my mother. They were always friends, you recall."

This was the strangest bit of the conversation of all—him speaking of her mother and his in eternal tête-à-tête. How much had passed between the old friends since Marianne had left Lincolnshire? Was her mother's hair still graying brown, or had it gone white? Did she still refrain from taking the sugar in her tea that she loved but had declined while Marianne's father, kind but ascetic, was alive?

Marianne's thoughts always came back to food now. Surely that was a sign she was where she ought to be.

When Sally returned, arms full of the ingredients for the cheese sauce, Marianne was not sorry to turn to the stove. To the work she knew and understood as she did nothing else.

Occasionally, she peeked into the refectory as the young ladies took their dinner. She did so today, reminding herself that she was where she belonged: in the kitchen, as a cook.

She could have existed always apart from the upstairs, never seeing the young ladies or knowing whether they enjoyed the work of the kitchens. But she liked seeing them, liked knowing most of them bolted their food with healthy young appetites and took second helpings. The understandable hunger that a girl in her teens developed after racking her brain all day overlaid even the lessons in deportment and manners.

Before taking their food, the girls always said their prayers, then a chant, sort of a school motto, though Marianne had never seen it anywhere official.

*I am an exceptional young lady. I deserve the best and am prepared for the worst. Whatever comes my way, I am equal to the task. I know that I am never alone, because my teachers and sisters will always watch out for me as I watch out for them.*

They all wore the same outfit, a pretty if simple gown of a medium blue color that was almost universally flattering, but they were hardly birds of a feather. The young ladies were any age from eight to twenty, magpies and peacocks and sparrows and ravens. Some sang, some imitated, some flaunted. Some eyed their surroundings, biding.

All eating, though, and with relish.

And Marianne felt lonely as she watched them dine. She'd never gone away to school. But once, thus, she had sat with her sisters, and they had been so different, but all belonged together.

It had been too long since she'd written to them. Both well-dowered due to the sale of the family lands, they'd married—she assumed happily—and had some children. She'd never met them, but the news was good. It was good enough.

She hadn't noticed the empty seat at the head of the table until a woman's voice sounded at her side. "Mrs. Redfern. Come and speak with me in my office."

Faintly Welsh-accented and not to be gainsaid, this was the unmistakable tone of the headmistress.

Unworried but puzzled, Marianne eased shut the servants' door and followed her employer up the back stairs, then out into a wide and bright corridor along which Mrs. Brodie's office was located. As the older woman eased behind her desk, covered with tidy stacks of correspondence and other administrative papers, Marianne stood with hands folded neatly behind her back.

A small woman in her middle forties giving an impression of great strength, the headmistress was dressed all in black. Her hair, black too, though shot with gray, was severely pinned back from a face that would never not be beautiful.

When she settled a few papers, she looked up at Marianne. "Sit, sit. If you wish. I need to discuss a few items related to the..." She smiled. "Donor Dinner, I believe the staff are calling it?"

Marianne returned the headmistress's smile as she sat in the indicated chair. "Quickest way of reminding ourselves what we're all working for."

There was much more to the event than the food, though that was Marianne's only concern. But she knew that the older students would be exhibiting their more conventional talents, with needlework and artwork on display, with recitations in French and English, with sentences parsed and history recited. The food was the backdrop; the girls were the performers. And all of it was to convince well-meaning, deep-pocketed sorts that Mrs. Brodie's Academy was worth funding.

Mrs. Brodie jotted notes on a slip of foolscap that she slid across the desk to her. Certain wines to be served before dinner, along with the first of the exhibitions. This would require an adjustment to the wines served during dinner, which would in turn require a different order of dishes in the courses. Marianne nodded, understanding, already imagining the switch and slide of roasts and sides in her plan for the first course.

This office was another place she belonged, and her employer's trust in her was proof. And because of that, she'd do anything in her power—and maybe a little beyond—to make this dinner a success.

She'd been hired eight years before not because she was right for the post, but because she was desperate and admitted it. Upon leaving Lincolnshire, she had tried to find work elsewhere in London, only to realize she had no useful skills. She had stopped at Mrs. Brodie's Academy because of the gilded plate on the front of the building denoting the name of the place. Run by a woman, she'd thought. More likely to be safe; less likely to have leering eyes and pinching hands.

Carrying a valise and dressed in her last clean gown, her last pair of clean gloves, and her best hat, she'd rung the front bell, bold as anything. "I have an appointment with the headmistress."

The butler looked at her doubtfully. "Your name?"

Her mind reeled. Should she make something up? She could think of no falsity that would make her more likely to gain an appointment. Mrs. Brodie would never believe she was Princess Charlotte.

"Miss Redfern," she said crisply and honestly. And when she was ushered into the headmistress's office, to her surprise, delight, and simultaneous terror, the honesty continued.

Behind the big desk sat the small woman, a little less gray then, but no less forceful or beautiful. With a dark and steady stare, Mrs. Brodie asked, "Why have you said you have an appointment with me?"

"I need a job," Marianne blurted. "And I hoped… I would rather not be pinched and violated. I thought perhaps with a woman in charge…"

"Very reasonable," the older woman said in a crisp voice tinged with the accent of Wales. She regarded Marianne for a long moment, up and down. Marianne made herself as still as a statue, imagining herself at a dance waiting for someone to invite her to the floor. At last, the headmistress gave a little nod. "What skills have you?"

"The usual useless ones. Needlework and watercolor. But I will do any honest thing," she added quickly.

"Why limit yourself?" Marianne must have gaped, for the headmistress lifted a hand and said, "Very well, we will try you in the kitchen. If you sew and paint, you must be good with your hands, and Cook will welcome a new assistant. If you are eager to learn, you will do well. And if you are not..." Mrs. Brodie shrugged. "If you only want a safe place to live and honest work to do, the academy will take you on as a maid or find a similar post for you."

Now that the different options were dangled before her, Marianne found that *any honest thing* had lost its appeal. Being a housemaid when one could be a cook's assistant? The latter was clearly more exciting. It was hardly the dream she'd once had for her life, but those dreams had relied upon others. Those dreams were done and gone.

"I would like to assist the cook," Marianne told Mrs. Brodie. "I will do my best to learn from her."

"I believe you will." Mrs. Brodie named a wage that sounded a pittance compared to her former pin money. But it was generous compared to the maid's wages she'd been offered at other places—and with no pinching or harassment. "If you accept, you can have your things sent and begin tomorrow."

"I have no other things," said Marianne.

Mrs. Brodie lifted her brows. "Then we'd best get you a uniform. And you can start work at once. My girls and staff eat well here. One cannot learn or do one's best work if one is hungry."

A footman guided her through the academy, giving her a bit of a tour on their way to the kitchens. Marianne regarded the students closely as she got the opportunity, wondering what an exceptional young lady looked like. To her eye, they looked like every other girl and young woman of her acquaintance. Some were quite pretty, some plain. Some had dark skin, some light. Some looked at the world as if it were a celebration. Some passed through the corridors in dreamy silence.

She wished she knew what to say to them. How to warn them against hoping for too much. But the words caught in her throat; it wasn't her place to say anything to these girls, whose fees ran the school and paid her own salary.

Her place was not what it had once been.

But after eight years at the academy, she had made the place her own, and she was proud to have done so.

"And how is the new kitchenmaid working out?" Mrs. Brodie asked now, her voice tinged with humor. "Mr. Grahame, is that right?"

Mrs. Brodie always had names right. "We'll still need a new kitchenmaid in the long term," Marianne answered. "But Mr. Grahame's help means I won't have to hire someone while we're preparing for the dinner."

"Very good. I'll leave the hiring up to Mrs. Hobbes," said Mrs. Brodie of the housekeeper, "and will instruct her to get your approval on all kitchen staff. And I will trust that Mr. Grahame will know his place."

The words reflected Marianne's own thoughts, making her smile. "I'll see to it that he does." For he was at her side each day, at last, and that night, she would have him in her bed again.

Perhaps she could even persuade him to stay.

## Chapter Six

Three days until the Donor Dinner, and if Jack hadn't come to London to help, Marianne knew she'd be tearing her hair out.

Not that he'd come to London specifically to help her. But still, it had all worked out for the best. He was a part of her life again and more essential every day.

April had crashed into May with a wave of heat, making meal preparations an ordeal of perspiration and hurry. The stolen hours of rest were slow and cool and sweet in comparison.

Jack was with Marianne now, sitting at the long worktable in the slow hours of early afternoon when luncheon was complete and the final preparations for dinner still ahead. It was the last moment of leisure they'd take, probably, until the grand dinner was past.

He'd asked about her favorite things to cook, and she pleased herself by giving him a thorough answer. Settling them each with a great mug of tea laced with honey—she'd made use of that honeycomb after all—she paged through her book of handwritten recipes and notes to show him some of her favorites.

"This was the first dinner I ever prepared as cook, head of the kitchen, after Mrs. Patchett retired." She pushed back her cap to scratch at her hairline, remembering the heat and panic of that day. "Underdone lamb and a jumble of over-roasted vegetables. You see how many notes I made about the ovens? Each has a personality of its own. If I ever move on to a new kitchen, I'll have to learn the ovens all over again."

Jack sipped from his mug, brows arching quizzically. "Overdone and underdone, and that was one of your favorite things to cook?"

"Hardly a triumph, you mean?" She smiled. "At the time, it was horrid, but in hindsight, I'm quite proud of it. The young ladies probably didn't enjoy eating it, but it fed them all the same. By making that meal, I realized I could do the job here of cook, even if I wasn't doing it as well as I wanted to."

Jack drew the book toward him and looked over the notes. "There's no question you can do the job now. I've never eaten so well as I have this past week and a half."

"Flatterer."

He grinned. "Sometimes I am, but not at the moment." He drank more tea, turned a page. "Chocolate cream tarts? Big masculine creature that I am, I shall swoon at the sight of this recipe. Why do you not make those every day?"

A surprise for Mrs. Brodie's birthday two years before. Those *had* been fun to make—and to sample. "Any pleasure can get wearisome, even chocolate cream. But it's been too long since I made them. Maybe I can include a tower of them in the dessert course at the Donor Dinner." Her fingers flexed for a pencil and her foolscap sheets of planned-out courses.

A warm hand overlaid her own. "No. Please. I didn't mean for you to add more work to your endless list. I was merely envying those past people who were able to taste your tarts."

"That sounds like a smutty joke."

"Good. It was meant to." He leaned closer, speaking into her ear. "And grateful I am that I've been able to taste your—"

"*Stop*," she hissed, looking around the kitchen. Sally was stocking supplies, moving about from larder to pantry to worktable, and might overhear anything, anytime.

He arranged his expression into one of great sobriety. "Stopping now. Perfectly proper. Didn't mean anything smutty."

Marianne drank from her own mug of tea to cover a smile.

"Changing the subject to one of which you might approve." Jack nodded toward the cook's assistant, just entering the kitchen from the meat safe. "I see Sally carries a book of her own in her apron pocket. Hullo, Sally."

The younger woman was carrying in the head of a hog on a great platter. As she set it at the end of the table, she replied, "Mrs. Redfern told me what a good practice it was to have a pocket book and pencil at all times. A cook might need to write any sort of note about a recipe or an ingredient, and it saves time never having to hunt up paper and pen."

"Exactly right." Marianne beamed at her. Even the hog's head seemed to smile from its dish, as if pleased that it had finished brining.

"Mrs. Redfern, I'll get the stockpot ready for the head," replied Sally. This sentence likely made little sense to Jack, but Marianne understood it to mean that her assistant would collect the needed vegetables and seasonings and bring them to a boil.

"Remember to add trotters, or the brawn won't thicken," Marianne instructed. "A half dozen should do. And remove and quarter the ears before you put the head in."

Sally bobbed her head, understanding, and retrieved a shining pot from its place. She passed into the scullery to fill it with water.

"You're a fine teacher," Jack said. "Did you ever think of offering lessons in the evening, like Miss Carpenter does?"

"Oh. I don't know." Marianne glanced at the hog's head. It still appeared pleased. "I do like teaching, but I've never thought of working with someone outside of my own kitchen."

"Surely cookery is as useful a skill as what you've learned from Miss Carpenter." He rubbed at his shoulder with a persecuted expression.

"Cooking's different." She wrinkled her nose. "It doesn't have the excitement of throwing an assailant to the ground."

Jack raised his eyes to the plaster ceiling. "There is a hog's head staring at me from the end of the table, and she says cooking isn't exciting."

She laughed. "That's for making brawn, and it's only here for another minute. Though if you don't know the reason, I suppose it does lend the kitchen an air of mystery."

"Or grisliness."

"Or that," she granted. "Maybe Miss Carpenter's fighting is the same as teaching lessons myself. If I'd never tried it, I'd think I could never do it."

"Which means you're all prepared to become a wonderful teacher as soon as you try it out."

"But if I were to teach…" She looked at the hog's head. The book of handwritten notes. Neither offered her insight. "I'd have less time for cooking." *Or being with you.*

She wasn't sorry when Sally swooped by, picked up the head, and strode back to the stockpot with it.

"When we gain something," Jack said, more serious than he'd seemed yet today, "something else is lost. I believe this completely."

Marianne considered. "I suppose that's true. As I gained cooking knowledge, I lost my satisfaction with the way I grew up. It's no longer enough for me to embroider and watercolor and smile. Those skills did me no good, and all the while I was building them, I didn't know how helpless I was becoming."

"That is not such a bad thing to lose, then."

"It's not." She added more quietly, "I've lost more too. I've lost my faith that the way things have been is the way they have to be."

He nodded at her prized book. "You are talking about more than the method of spicing a joint of meat, aren't you?"

"Of course I am."

Though it wasn't spices that had got her thinking of *what we've always done* versus *what could be*. It was the pages of sauces.

Ever since she had begun learning cookery, Marianne had loved sauces. They were like clothing for food, turning the plain into the special. The bland into the savory.

Mrs. Patchett had been fond of traditional English fare, and certainly Marianne preferred good fresh ingredients that didn't need to be hidden by vinegar and salt. But a sauce! Oh! It turned a good saddle of mutton into a roast that popped with the flavors of heavy meat, floral herbs, pungent garlic. It awoke the nose as well as the mouth. It not only fed people, it made them smile.

She'd spent some of her wages on books of recipes from France, then translated them with her schoolroom French and the help of Mademoiselle Gagne, the French instructor. Many of those notes had made their way into the book, now open and vulnerable before Jack. She'd made that book without him, when she'd never expected to see him again. When she had accepted that.

She'd been all right on her own because she'd had to be. Now, though she'd gained Jack, she'd lost that feeling of solid independence.

"I'd best get back to work," she said. "Dinner will need its sauces." She drained her tea, then pushed back her chair. As she stood, she tucked her book back into her apron pocket.

Jack stood too, catching her hand before she could step away. "You're talking about more than food, you said. Are you talking about us? Is the way we are now the way we always have to be?"

"Kitchenmaid and cook?" she joked, though she knew that was not what he meant. On her hands, tough with old nicks and burns and scars, his fingers were warm and strong.

"That's not only up to me," she dodged, remembering their first night together in her tiny chamber. So much about them had never been up to only them.

"It's not," he agreed. Bending his head toward hers, he spoke low into her ear. "But I've already decided what I want. It's you, Marianne, and I would lo—"

"Mrs. Redfern," piped up Evans, the errand boy, as he darted into the room. "The new kitchenmaids are here. Where do you want them?"

Marianne shook her hand free of Jack's grasp, tipped her ear away from his voice. She had hardly taken in what he'd said, and now Evans wasn't making any sense. "New kitchenmaids? I didn't—"

"Show them in," Jack interrupted. When she looked at him quizzically, he didn't return her gaze.

Four kitchenmaids, straight from an agency, filed into the room and stood in a line along the end of the table. They were all wide-eyed, a stair-step of tidy young women not the slightest bit like Jack Grahame.

And Marianne didn't know her own kitchen anymore. With the arrival of the kitchenmaids, something had indeed been lost. The space, the sense of familiarity. The notion that she was in charge of decisions made here.

She turned to Jack, and she didn't quite know him either. He'd lost his humor and become square-shouldered and stern, hands folded behind his back.

"You seem to know what's happening here," she said. "Why is that? And why is it that I don't?"

He still didn't look at her. Everyone seemed to be waiting for someone else to speak.

So Marianne spoke again, annoyance warring with puzzlement. "You've already decided what you want, you said. What have you decided, Mr. Grahame?"

It was bad timing, the kitchenmaids arriving just as Jack was attempting to tell Marianne how he felt—preparatory, he hoped, to convincing her his next choice was the right one. But maybe there was no timing that would have been good enough for that.

"Miss White," Jack raised his voice, recalling Sally from the stove where she'd just stirred the contents of the stockpot. "Take charge for a few minutes, please."

"Mrs. Redfern," he addressed Marianne, then tugged her away from the new arrivals and into her chamber, lit the lamp, shut the door. Instead of cozy, the room felt cramped and close. The scent of laundry soap and lamp oil was strong.

"Let me explain," he began.

"Please do," she said. "Because you just ordered me about in my own kitchen, and in front of four new maids that I certainly did not hire."

Her voice was firm and dignified, tinged with hurt, and he felt like a villain.

Which was ridiculous, because she ought to see him as a hero. "I hired them myself from a reputable agency, because you need more hands for the Donor Dinner." He really had to say it all. "Because I can't stay as kitchenmaid any longer. My mother wrote me that she's ill. I've already got my carriage ready. I only waited to leave until the maids arrived from the agency."

And postponed telling her of his departure in favor of tea and fantasies of chocolate tarts. Because he knew she wouldn't like it that he was leaving; he didn't like it either.

"So you've known all day that you are leaving." She folded her arms—not in defiance, but as if she were holding herself together.

"My mother is ill," he said again. "That is the more important part of what I just said."

Her green eyes caught his. "Gravely ill?"

"I don't know. If she were, she wouldn't tell me. I just don't *know*." How powerless he felt, his loved ones scattered like sand. He wished he could gather them all up and keep them close to his heart. *Be well, stay by me.*

She pressed at her temples, a gesture he recognized as her sorting-out-a-plan maneuver. For an instant, he took hope that she was thinking up a way to come along, to lend comfort to a woman she'd always been fond of.

"I hope she will be well," Marianne said. "Of course you must go, and give her all my best. But, Jack—"

"You could come along," he blurted. "That is, you could come after the Donor Dinner. Visit your mother."

She looked around at her room. "Oh. No, I—no. I don't want to go back."

Which was different from, *I can't go back.* He wasn't sure which was better.

"Are you certain of that?" he pressed. "Two years you've been in this room as cook, and there's not a drawing or book or trinket to show it's yours. This looks like the room of someone who's ready to leave, Marianne."

She lifted her brows, looking piqued. "It's not. It's the room of someone who expects to be left and who will get away before she has to bear the humiliation of it."

He understood what she meant. It all went back to eight years ago, when they'd been split apart. He tried pacing, gave up at the small width of the room, and stood before her. "Eight years ago, did you truly want to come to London? Or did you just want to get away from me?"

Her mouth opened. Not a single word came out.

"I see," he said. "You can't give me an answer, which tells me right enough what it is."

"Jack, all that was so long ago." She stretched out a hand, the one he'd held just a few minutes ago.

"It was, and yet it seems we're not done with it." He'd never considered before whether he blamed her for leaving Lincolnshire so abruptly, leaving him to deal with the sad families left behind.

It seemed he did. He didn't take her hand. As she let it fall to her side again, he spoke on.

"When the banns were called for Helena and me, you could have stayed in your father's home, but you were too proud and determined to do that, and you left for London. I think you don't do anything you don't want to, and you never will. I just wonder what you'll want next."

"Not to be left behind again," she mumbled.

He set his jaw. "Your family was left behind, not you. And you're not the only one who had losses.

"Your mother wanted me to go after you," he added. "Did you know that? She thought you'd be murdered on your way to London."

"Obviously, I didn't know that. And just as obviously, I wasn't murdered, and you didn't come after me."

"I did. It just took me a few years, until I could be proper about the matter."

"Proper." She laughed dryly. "Nothing we've done in this room has been proper."

"And how we've enjoyed it." He returned her smile, feeling it as a reprieve. "As you might guess, your father argued your mother out of her plans. You were almost of age, he said, and he knew you'd had your life shaken up. He told her he'd have friends of his in London check on you."

"Which friends?"

"Ah—I don't know. Does it matter?"

"I—no, not really. But I did go away, and I can't ask him now. I can't ask him anything ever again." She sank onto the bed, as if weighted by the years that had passed.

He crouched before her. "I couldn't have given up love, our love, for any reason but love. Not money, not greed, not security—nothing for myself, because with you I had enough. But for love of my family, I could. I had to."

"You made the sensible choice," she said. "I know that. We've discussed that." She looked at him with eyes like emeralds. Like spring lettuces, costing too dear. Like leaves on the trees he was missing. Like a mossy stone, perfect for skipping, on the banks of a pond near his home. "I haven't seen the sea in eight years either. At home, I would be able to go to the sea and put my feet in the sand."

*Home*. He pounced on this, thinking of what would appeal to a cook. "And collect mussels and catch fresh fish."

She rolled her eyes. "I would leave the catching to the fishermen, cold as the North Sea is. But you've a good thought. Cookery in different parts of England is—or could be—much different."

That hadn't been his thought at all, but he let her credit him for the insight. "Then you'll come with me?" He let himself hope.

"I was only musing. No, I won't be going back." She shook her head. "Will you be returning to me?"

God, this room was hot. How would she get any sleep in here tonight? "As soon as I'm able. Though I can't know when that would be, because of my mother's health. You must see that."

She laid a hand on his chest—to feel his heartbeat, he thought, but no, she was only pushing him back a small distance so she could rise from the bed. Jack stood, knees and ankles popping as he rose from his crouch. Yet another way the years had left their mark.

Her fingers became busy, tucking strands of hair beneath her cap. "What you've said ought to sound like a promise. But instead, I'm left wondering—when were you going to tell me you are leaving? All I have is my kitchen, Jack, and you made me look a fool in it." Her hands dropped, her voice lowered. "You made me feel foolish."

"I don't like telling you things you won't like." He knew this was the wrong thing to say as soon as the words left his mouth.

"Don't you? You don't like telling me you'll be leaving me for a perfectly understandable reason, or that you've hired a generous number of servants to replace you and make my job easier?"

"Well." When she put it that way, his thinking was stupid. "I was afraid that when I left early, it would remind you of eight years ago. And so I wanted to—"

"To make certain of it?" She rounded on him, filling the small room with her anger. "To make certain you caught me unawares, left me unprepared and gaping in the place I ought to feel safest? Hearing another's name called in the banns in church with yours. Having servants file into my kitchen expecting to be put to work. *Jack*."

She was shaking now. He reached out a hand to her, but she batted it away. "Jack," she said again, her voice cracking on the syllable. He hardly recognized the sound from lips that had spoken his name so many times. "Jack. Is this your way? Solve your problems at my expense? Buy your way out of a promise? Never tell me a truth you think I won't like, until it can't be ignored and it shatters my life?"

Clearly, they weren't talking only about the kitchenmaids anymore.

He shouldn't feel as if he were in the wrong, should he, for leaving to visit his mother? Yet he did, because his departure was so much…more. There was always more, always another layer of emotion old and new.

Damn love, damn devotion. It was ridiculously complicated, and with all he had learned in life, he'd never mastered how to talk about it.

"You don't trust me," she said. "You don't trust me to understand. You don't trust me with the truth of your life. All we have is make-believe and strawberries."

Stung, he replied, "That's terribly unfair. We have cabbages too—all right, this isn't the time for a joke. But, Marianne, I've done what I thought best. My parents never loved each other, which is why my father was so adamant that I make a marriage for gain. My best friend ran off to London eight years ago and wrote to everyone but me. Those things are real, as real as this room. And if I hid the truth, it was because I couldn't bear to lose you."

"But you knew you would then. Wedding someone else has that effect." Her tone was dust-dry. "So really, yes, you didn't trust me to understand that you might have obligations to others besides me."

She moved past him to put a hand on the door's handle. "That was a large matter. This is a small one—at least, I hope it is, and your mother will recover. But if you don't trust me in matters large or small, then we haven't any foundation for being together. So you needn't return after all."

She sounded so cold. All business, as she might with a new kitchenmaid she wasn't sure she had any use for. And he realized, "You haven't really forgiven me, have you?"

She let her arm fall to her side. "You told me from the moment of your arrival that you aren't sorry for any choice you've made. If you're not apologizing, then what is there to forgive? There's no wrongdoing on either side. There's only what had to be then and what can't be now."

"What do you mean, it can't be?"

"I belong here. You belong there, three days' travel north, with your uncomfortable truths hidden in your pockets until they don't fit anymore. So it's clear that we don't belong together."

No. This couldn't be it. This couldn't be it. "You're ending it? After all this time waiting?"

"You haven't been waiting for me. The person who leaves isn't the one who waits, and you left me the moment you agreed to marry someone else." She smiled, but it was nothing like an expression of joy. "I left for London years ago. Now it's your turn to walk away. Odd how I am the one left behind, whether I depart or show you the door."

How was she so calm? He was a roiling mess of feelings that he couldn't put a name to. "You say that as if I mean nothing to you. When the kitchenmaids arrived"—damn those kitchenmaids—"I was trying to tell you how I feel about you. That you're my choice, and I love you."

"You are certainly free to do that. I can't change your feelings. Nor can I make you trust me, or think of the power you have when you hold someone's heart and dignity in your hands."

She turned her back to him, tracing the line in the door where two boards were joined.

"I hold your heart? But you never said—"

"Forget what I said or didn't say. What I'm saying now is what counts. I won't let you ruin another place for me. I won't place my trust where it isn't returned." She was turning the handle now. "I have a life here, one that I created myself, and I don't have to rely on you. I shouldn't have let myself do it at all."

"But I want you to. You can." He knew she would hear the words as hollow.

Indeed, she shook her head. "The only thing I ask of you is to leave if you've a mind to. And don't plan to come back again."

She opened the door of her chamber; the air of the kitchens was comparatively cool on his face. She pushed past him and, with skill and speed, took charge of the four new maids.

She didn't trust him anymore, and it was his own doing. If his heart was cracking into bits, that was his own doing too.

He drew himself up. Retrieved his hat and coat. And then, because he'd never been able to deny Marianne anything but his hand in marriage, he obeyed her wishes and left.

## Chapter Seven

After three days in his carriage, Jack was a mass of thwarted energy and wonderings and worries. As soon as the wheels turned from the main road and rolled past the low red-brick wall that edged this side of his property, he was knocking to his driver to pull up. Then he was opening the door, bounding down, arranging to have his things brought on to the main house, and haring off to the dower house.

The Grahames had always owned a great deal of land, though it hadn't produced well until the Wilcox money had allowed for improvements in drainage. Now, as the carriage trundled on along the graveled drive to Westerby Grange, he cut through tidy fields and passed beneath trees, fresh and spring green. Here and there, the land was still wild, and he slopped through the edge of a waterlogged fen. Thinking, wondering, with every pumping stride.

Had it been worth it, leaving London and Marianne? Was his mother well? Had he done right?

A small distance separated the dower house from the main building, and Jack's path had been the most direct. Let the carriage make its ponderous and proper way; he'd thunder through one more copse and—there! The smaller copy of the Grange was square and sturdy red brick, with a bowed front, and…and thank God, there was no black crepe swagged over the windows. If Mrs. Grahame was gravely ill, she yet survived.

He strode to the front entrance, now feeling every bit of the heavy sog of his abused boots, and caught his breath before he thumped the knocker. The butler who answered wore his usual uniform of severe black and white, his usual mien of unflappable politeness.

"Mr. Grahame, good afternoon," said Trilby. "May I say, sir, welcome home?"

"You may, with my thanks," Jack said, still slightly winded. "Is my mother well?"

"She is almost herself again." The butler stood aside to welcome Jack into the little entrance hall. Trilby, a long-loved and now elderly servant, had moved from the main house to the dower with Jack's mother upon his marriage. Jack trusted the old servant's report more than his own mother's account of her health, which was likely to be offhanded and vague so as not to worry him.

Perhaps he'd inherited that hide-the-troublesome-truth quality from his mother.

With Trilby's reassurance, Jack let out a great breath. It released the tension within him, though it left him hollow and dissatisfied. If he'd known…if he hadn't left London…

Would it have mattered? Or would he have ruined his chance with Marianne soon enough, in some similar way?

Trilby would never raise his brows or demonstrate impatience, but the way he hovered close was an unmistakable nudge. "Would you care to join Mrs. Grahame and Mrs. Redfern in the drawing room? Miss Grahame arrived perhaps ten minutes ago, and tea has just been served."

Miss Grahame—that meant his sister Viola. Maybe it was for the best that he'd walk in on all three women at once. He could greet them all, then leave with his duty done, and they could get on with their gossip about him.

Taking the hint from Trilby, Jack entered the drawing room and faced the trio of familiar faces that turned his way. There was Marianne's mother, Mrs. Redfern, a spare and tidy woman almost crippled by rheumatism, but still with the strong chin and bright eyes she'd bequeathed to her three daughters. Viola, Jack's elder sister, in her usual half mourning, with wide and shrewd gray eyes and her light hair in a low knot. And in her favorite chair, surrounded by cushions, was Jack's mother, as round and wrinkled as an apple beginning to show its age and still just as rosy. Her once-black hair was now heavily salted with white, and it curled as tightly as Jack's would if he didn't keep it cropped short.

True to the butler's word, she looked well enough. She was tired, that was clear from the cushions supporting her, but her hands on her cup and saucer were steady. Her voice, when she greeted Jack, was clear.

And then began the interrogation.

"Jacob Elias, you've come all alone?" She craned her neck to look behind him. "No Marianne with you?"

Jacob, ugh. Elias, double ugh. "I rushed back to see how you were," Jack explained. "Marianne still had work to do in London."

Mrs. Redfern's shoulders sank. "I'd wished to see her again, very much."

She wasn't the only one, though all three women knew that. Jack had journeyed to London on impulse, he thought, but not a one of these widows had seemed surprised by his plans. Instead, they'd all told him a more ladylike version of, *It's about damned time*, and, *Put a ring on her finger*, and, *You sapskull*.

"Why on *earth* are you here without her?" Jack's mother asked. "I was only sending you news. I didn't ask you to return home. Why didn't you just write?"

"What does my daughter look like now?" asked Mrs. Redfern. "Is she well? Did she send you with a letter for me?"

"What did you do to ruin things with Marianne?" Viola demanded.

Jack rolled his eyes. "Can't I have tea and cakes before you sling all these questions at me?"

"Fine," said his mother. "But you have to sit on the jackal."

Strange though it sounded, this statement made perfect sense to Jack. His mother, flush with funds and independence all at once, had completely redecorated the dower house in Egyptian style a few years before. Her chair, striped in a bright gold and blue silk, nestled in a corner of the small drawing room. Near at hand was a scroll-back settee of startling crimson on which perched the other two women. Which meant the only other place to sit was on the larger-than-life seated jackal of black-painted wood.

Not for the first time, Jack sat on the back of his near-namesake and patted its pricked ears. "Two sugars, please, Mother," he said. "I'm tired out from the trip. And in answer to your questions—as you see, Marianne's not with me. Mrs. Redfern, she's well and strong and beautiful, and she cooks like a dream, and I'm a villain for not getting a letter from her.

"And I didn't write for news, Mother, because...I wanted to see for myself that you were all right." He'd come to see how his mother did, just as he'd gone to London to see Marianne. He didn't want to write to people when he could see them for himself.

He just wished he hadn't had to leave one person behind to see the others.

She handed over his tea with a smile. "It's a good thing you cared enough to come. I had a few bad days of it and complained unendingly."

"You weren't *that* bad," allowed Mrs. Redfern. "But there are many reasons to be grateful you've recovered."

"You haven't answered my question," Viola said. "What have you done wrong?"

"Why must I have done anything wrong?" He gulped tea, taking strength from its heat and sweetness. "How do you know we're not betrothed and I'm not deliriously happy?"

All three women looked at him in pointed silence.

After a moment, he relented. Balancing his cup beside him on the jackal's back, he said, "She thinks I don't trust her. So she's done with me."

All three women looked at him in accusing silence.

Viola was the first to break it. Sighing heavily, she stood, which meant Jack did also. "Walk me back to the Grange," she said. "You can explain everything on the way."

"I want to know all the gossip!" cried their mother.

"We'll get it later," soothed Mrs. Redfern. "Either Viola will tell us, or I'll write to Marianne and hear her side."

"Or you could leave it be." Jack retrieved his cup, drained his tea, then set cup and saucer on the tea tray. "And trust that I did my best and don't want to talk about it anymore."

All three women looked at him in surprised silence. Then, as if cued by a conductor, they all hooted with laughter. Jack recalled the feeling of being flipped and pummeled during one of Miss Carpenter's lessons.

"Come on, we'll walk back before you make a fool of yourself." Viola took Jack's arm. Bidding the older women farewell, they left the little house and stepped out into the blueing evening light.

Days were long in May, for which he was grateful. He'd arrived in daylight, able to blunder across his own land, able to orient himself to the familiar space of it. As if he'd never gone to London, given his heart anew, chopped cabbage, tried to set a new course for his life. Bought strawberries and honeycomb. Hunted for a bit of the past he'd thought he'd lost.

Their footsteps crunched on the neat gravel path. Jack bent to pluck a weed that interrupted the smooth, pale surface.

When he straightened, Viola looked at him quizzically. "It's my responsibility," he said. It was all his responsibility. Just as the Donor Dinner—that was today, wasn't it?—was Marianne's and Mrs. Brodie's.

They were where they belonged.

"Sorry I got Mother and Mrs. Redfern laughing at you," Viola said when Jack took her arm again. Their pace was slow, as if neither of them wanted to arrive at their destination. "I thought they'd ask you fewer questions if they took your arrival lightly. Neither of them's been well, you know."

"I know." Mrs. Redfern had been in pain for years, unable to travel beyond the nearby hamlet. Certainly unable to go to London and visit her absent daughter. And his own mother—well, her health had been worn into his brain for days. "It's all right. Just…don't start laughing again yourself."

"I wouldn't." Viola looked thinner since he'd left more than a fortnight before, but peaceful. Calm. Her smile was ready and knowing, as if she'd come to some decision Jack had yet to realize was facing him. "But I am surprised you left London without a promise from Marianne. So long, I lived in your house with the love you couldn't have. I thought you'd want to do the same to me."

"There's no revenge of that where love is concerned." His boots were dark on the gravel, each step square and careful. "I'd never have wished you a widow, Vee. I know you still miss her."

She caught the gray lace at her throat. "Yes," she said simply. "You might be the only one who knows how much."

A spinster sister living with a newly married couple was ordinary enough. For that spinster to love the bride, though, and vice versa, was thought unnatural by many. In public, Viola's grief had to be that of a sister, a friend. In private, Jack had let her cry on his shoulder as often as she'd needed to. He could never envy her loss, but he did envy her devotion. No one would shed so many tears over him. No one existed for him to weep over as if he'd lost his heart.

Maybe that was not such a bad thing. Some part of Jack had always longed for Marianne, his missing piece. Briefly made whole again, he'd been cleaved anew. He would need far more than a few days to forget that time at her side.

Was it better to forget? Or to be changed?

"I have been thinking," Viola said, "that I should like to move households."

Ah. So this was the decision behind that beatific smile. "Surely not to live with Mother?"

Viola's expression of horror was eloquent. "Indeed not. I love visiting her, but living with her would make me only a daughter again. I've altered too much for that."

Jack nodded, accepting. "What have you in mind?"

"A cottage, maybe. Not like a tenant. I don't know how to do anything useful. But a cottage of my own, where I won't be surrounded by…so much."

After two years, she was ready to break from the constant reminders of loss in the house she and Helena had shared. He could understand that. He could smile, even, at her assertion that she didn't know how to do anything useful. It reminded him of Marianne—and since those reminders were all too few here, he didn't want to escape them. Yet.

"You know how to make a home," Jack told his sister. "Nothing could be more useful for a woman who wants her own cottage. You find a place you like, and I'll buy it and deed it to you. Helena would like that, don't you think?"

"She would like to see us happy. And on an evening like this, how could we not be?" Viola lifted her face to the sky, breathing in deeply.

To Jack, the air smelled clean and cool. The sky was big and open, poked gently by treetops. There were the croplands, their earth rich and smooth and well tended. The wolds, high and rolling and treed, and the fens to balance, grassy and waterlogged and teeming with buntings and crickets and butterflies. The sun began to yawn gold and pink across the deepening blue above.

It was nothing like London.

He'd gone to find the man he used to be. He'd gone to feel something, to be absolved. And he had placed all that responsibility on Marianne's shoulders, though he swore he wanted nothing from her.

He'd always wanted something from her. He had always wanted her to love him. When he tried to make himself into the sort of man he'd always wanted to be, it was because that was the sort of man he'd grown up admiring. Just as she'd been swaddled in silks and taught to paint and sew and flirt, his examples had been men who mended fences—literally and figuratively. Men who rode and learned and were accomplished at everything from Latin to getting a muddy field to produce. And never, in all those years, had anything made him as happy as learning to cook had made Marianne.

When she went away, she'd learned who she wanted to be. Never yet had Jack sorted out so much. He'd come all the way from Lincolnshire to London hoping she'd solve his problems. Hoping she'd make it all right that he'd spent the years away from her by leaping, now, into his arms.

But neither of them was the same as they'd been eight years before, when she might have leaped—but he wouldn't have been able to catch her. They were, deep down, the same people, but they knew better now. She wouldn't leap unless she knew she could land on her own, and he…here he stood with his arms empty.

It was what he'd earned. The reaping of the lonely life he'd sown, where he'd become a bounty to the people around him, but neglected to feed his own heart.

"Right," Jack agreed into the silence. "Right. I can be happy here." What was the alternative? Never feeling joy at all?

Viola looked at him sharply. "No. I'm sorry I said that. You don't have to be happy this evening. It's not a requirement, and there's no schedule you must follow."

But that didn't comfort. If he didn't have a schedule, how could he know he'd ever reach his goal?

Whatever the devil it was.

"Are you coming in?" Viola asked. They had reached the front door of the Grange, the old brick manor house.

"Not yet," Jack told his sister. "I'll be in by dark."

She nodded, then climbed the steps and entered the house.

It was the only home Jack had ever known, and it wasn't nearly the home it ought to have been. Not because of any flaw in the house, which had stood and abided generations of Grahames, but because of the people who had raised him.

Had Jack's father had any regrets? He had no more regretted a life without passionate love than he would have regretted the temperature of the North Sea. It hadn't been within his power. And Jack couldn't blame him for that any more than he'd have blamed the sea for being cold.

He split from the graveled path before the house, taking a less-worn but ever familiar track onto lands that had once belonged to Marianne's father. Now they were his.

Beehives and all.

The hives were cultivated in sawed-off logs mounted upright, a shortened forest abuzz at this hour with bees returning for the night. On top of some were little house-shaped structures, a newer sort of hive hinged and cunningly divided so the nest would form up the middle and the honey and combs be constructed along the sides.

The bees were dedicated and predictable. This was what made them survive.

He'd been dedicated and predictable too, to Marianne. He'd reacted to protect himself, to hoard the little drops of honey, because he thought he'd never get more.

The things he'd done with the past eight years were good. Though he didn't give a damn about Latin and would happily forget it, he liked the fitness of his body, the quick understanding of the problems his land developed. He liked being able to understand when people were talking about him in another language, as if it were a secret code. He wouldn't end these things.

But they weren't enough—not for others, but for him. And if he wasn't enough for himself, how could he ever be enough for Marianne?

He hadn't really become the sort of man he wanted to be, the sort who trusted he could have what he wanted. The things money couldn't buy.

The things one had to deserve, to earn. The things one couldn't win with a bribe of a treat, or a week and a half of hard work and deep pleasures.

The things one received by being present, by being real, by being devoted and honest and true.

Marianne was right: He'd tried to buy his way out of the trouble he'd foreseen. And in doing so, he'd earned himself a problem entirely new.

He watched the bees find their hives. Homing in, knowing their place. But if their hive was upset, they'd build a new comb. Store more honey. They wouldn't give up; if they did, they wouldn't live.

There were worse examples. Even if his figurative hive lacked a queen.

So he thought about where he'd been most content. Not happy, brilliant and flashing, but content. Surviving and living and growing. Doing good.

And the answer was: with his hands in the dirt, making it easier for something to grow. With someone to talk to all the while at his side about anything from life's deepest questions to whether that cloud looked like a naked breast.

Ah, well. His lover and best friend lived in London now. She'd chosen London over him, cooking over home, the academy girls over her mother. That was her choice, and it angered him not to be chosen, but he had to forgive it. Without needing her to apologize for it, because she'd the right to make it.

But maybe he could bring a little of London to Lincolnshire. There had to be more women like her, like Viola, who wanted to learn more than they had. Daughters of impoverished merchants and tradespeople, too fine for service but unlikely to wed. Women who wanted to stand on their own.

One might even call them exceptional young ladies.

He wouldn't stop hoping for the return of the queen, but he couldn't force her to love him. To choose him. So he planned something else.

And he told the bees, in that old tradition, and asked for their blessing and their joy.

## Chapter Eight

Shortly before midnight, Marianne pressed a hand to the small of her aching back and saw the last dish stowed by the scullery maid. She bade the girl good night, sending her up to the attic quarters with a candle, then took a moment to admire the newly peaceful room in solitude.

After three days of frantic activity, the kitchen was calm again. Dark, save for Marianne's lamp and a crescent smile of moon through the high-up window. Clean from flagged floor to plaster ceiling. The staff was proud but weary to the bone.

And they would all be up early to make breakfast and do the whole round of meals and chores again, and yet again.

The Donor Dinner had come off without a hitch—as far as the guests knew, and that was good enough for Marianne. They'd never know the burnt-cream tarts were supposed to have spun sugar on their candied tops, but that it had all melted away. They'd never know that they'd been meant to have brawn, but it hadn't set properly, and so instead, the shreds of meat were fried to a crispy hash and stuffed beneath the pheasant's skin.

And they'd never know that the cook had overseen her assistant and four kitchenmaids with only half her mind on the task and her heart entirely absent.

It didn't help that the four maids Jack had hired were named Jane, Joan, Jill, and Jenny. Honestly! Names could start with letters other than J.

Marianne had peeped at the arriving guests, timing the readiness of dishes with the arrivals of the final couples. The men Mrs. Brodie invited had come in superfine and patent leather, with signet rings and gold fobs and generous bellies and loud laughs. The women had been in silks and jewels and feathers, their finery casting the glittering serving dishes into shade.

Elegant and wealthy as they all were, they were still people with appetites. The first polite demurrals past, they ate their food with the same eagerness the academy's young ladies demonstrated. The footmen reported to the kitchen each time they came for new dishes. The guests had finished the first course down to the bones; they had drunk the wines, then eaten yet more, then drunk an absolutely amazing amount.

The performances had been a success too, reported the footmen, from the sweetly framed needlework and watercolor paintings, to the recitations of poetry and translations from French. This last had been the cause of much amusement, as the students in

French were given random phrases and sentences by the guests. As more and more wine was imbibed, the suggestions grew increasingly ridiculous. When Mademoiselle Gagne's prize student composed an ode in French to the remains on a lady's plate—a stalk of asparagus, the delicate bones of a quail, and a few droplets of spilled wine—the company had agreed that such an effort could not be topped.

Next year, they'd all try to top it, though. And somehow they would.

Just now, the notion made Marianne tired.

No—*everything* made her tired. She was damned tired. Since her work was finally done, she could have her bed in her own room.

Lamp in hand, she dragged the small distance to her chamber—only to find the door open, a lit lamp already within, and a quiet figure awaiting her.

She squinted at the shadow and glare, recognizing the headmistress. "Mrs. Brodie? Is everything well?"

"Yes, very well. I only wanted to speak with you about our grand event."

Marianne set her lamp beside the other on the washstand, then glanced around the small space. "Ah—have a seat on the bed, if you wish? I'm sorry there's no chair."

"There's not much of anything in here." The older woman settled herself on the narrow bed, her back as straight as if she were seated on an antique fauteuil. "You look as if you are planning to leave the academy at a moment's notice."

"My room always looks like this," Marianne excused. "I only sleep in here." She bent her knees a tad, pressing her lower back against the wall to relieve its ache. Just being able to lean, not to hold up her own weight for a moment, was a relief.

"I see," said Mrs. Brodie. Not in the polite way a woman might accept a small confidence over tea, but in a quiet way, a slow and understanding way. As if she'd realized something that Marianne didn't intend her to.

For her two years as cook, she'd occupied this room without noticing its lack or loneliness—or her own. Yet they'd been obvious to Jack. They were obvious too, it seemed, to the headmistress.

But that was all Mrs. Brodie said on the subject. "The dinner was a great success, and the credit must go to your food and to the teachers who prepared the students so well." When she named the amount raised in subscriptions and donations, Marianne's eyes widened.

"You'll be able to accept more scholarship students," she realized.

"I will. And I'll have to raise fees for the next year; so many inquired about having their daughters attend." She smiled, standing. "I should let you get to bed. Morning will come early for us all, and the girls will be wanting breakfast."

On her feet, she hardly reached Marianne's cheekbone. Yet she extended a hand, placed it on Marianne's cheek, as comforting as a mother. "You do your best for us. Every meal, every day. Thank you for that, Mrs. Redfern."

Marianne's eyes watered. She squeezed them closed. "It's not enough."

"Not enough for what? Not enough for a cook to feed everyone at an academy?"

*Not enough for me to be proud of myself. Not enough to go home.*

Because she couldn't go home until she did so in triumph. And that was the one thing she could never feel until she *did* return. Until she felt forgiven herself. *You're not the only one who had losses*, Jack had told her, and she'd been the cause of them.

Mrs. Brodie stepped away. Marianne heard the rattle of the older woman's lamp. She opened her eyes to see the headmistress, aglow with light from the lamp she held. "You are an exceptional young lady."

Marianne dashed at her eyes. "It's in the name of the academy. They all are."

"Yes, they all are. There is no such thing as an ordinary young lady, because each is a human entirely unique." The older woman tipped her head, as lovely as a Madonna painting. "And that includes you. Don't you think your kitchenmaid always knew that? Not the newest ones, but the erstwhile Mr. Grahame?"

*Each is a human entirely unique.* The simple sentence, spoken with calm, struck Marianne like a thunderbolt.

She'd faulted Jack for placing his family's needs above her, hadn't she? Even though she knew they didn't balance. She was just one person, and they were many. But it wasn't a matter of mathematics or weight. It was a matter of people, and each was worthy.

To Jack, Marianne was. That was why he'd come to London—when he'd thought maybe, just maybe, she'd think him worthy of her.

And she'd sent him away. Just as she had cut herself off from her own family, all because of her own anger and humiliation.

"I'm not proud of what I've become," Marianne said in a choked voice.

Mrs. Brodie shrugged. "Maybe not all of it, no. I could tell you what I've done to survive, and you'd think—well. That's a story for another time." She looked thoughtfully at the lamp's globe, rubbing at a smut on the glittering glass. "But whatever comes, you're equal to the task. Isn't that something to be proud of?"

*I deserve the best and am prepared for the worst. Whatever comes my way, I am equal to the task.*

She'd heard this daily from the young ladies, believing it idly. But she hadn't *known* it until Jack appeared at the tradesmen's entrance of the servants' quarters with a little basket of strawberries in hand. Until he was part of her life again, and then wasn't.

He'd hidden a truth she couldn't possibly argue with, that he wanted to visit his sick mother, and he cared about helping Marianne make a success of the Donor Dinner. Those things were...sweet. Thoughtful. If he hadn't hidden his betrothal to Helena Wilcox eight years before, she wouldn't have thought anything of it. She'd have chided him for the surprise of four new maids, then come around to thanking him.

But they had a history, and his swift and sudden betrothal had been part of it. The now was never just now; it was the result of everything that had come before. Their present was too new to overlay the past, and so the past had cracked through. And though she'd forgiven him for it, what was the point in forgiving him again if he hadn't changed?

Or had he?

By hiding his betrothal until the humiliating truth came out in public, he'd spared himself alone. But by hiring four kitchenmaids to help Marianne, he'd spared *her*. He'd thought about what she would need in his absence. And she'd been vain to think she could do without extra help; all four of the Js, plus Marianne and Sally, had been busy since the moment of Jack's departure.

Oh, he was worthy. He was the best. But he'd never come to her again.

She'd have to go to him. To swallow her pride, and go home, and beg forgiveness.

If that was the worst, she was prepared to do it. She was equal to the task. She'd make everything right.

Mrs. Brodie was still looking at Marianne, now with a knowing curve to her lips. "Something to tell me?"

Marianne took a deep breath. Stood up straight, realizing she'd lost the heavy, exhausted feeling that had been weighing her down. "I need to beg leave of you, ma'am. To make a trip home as soon as is possible. It might be…quite a long leave."

"Very well. Will you be ready in the morning?"

Marianne blinked. Easy as that? "Oh—I—yes, of course! Though I hadn't meant to depart so soon and leave you without a cook."

"So you'll change the course of your life to spare me the trouble of contacting an agency? That's obliging of you."

Spluttering with surprised laughter, Marianne granted the truth of this. "Sally—Mrs. White—will do well as cook, I think, given more experience. You might like also to hire some of the new kitchenmaids on a permanent basis. They are all good workers."

"I'll ask Mrs. White"—the headmistress took on the new title seamlessly—"what she would prefer, in consultation with the housekeeper. And you are always welcome here. As a cook or, if you need any honest work, a chambermaid."

Marianne laughed. It was easier to laugh now. The easiest thing, now that there was something to do next besides cook, and cook. "I have some money awaiting me…I think." Her sisters had been dowered, but what had her mother done with Marianne's share of the money?

She'd never thought of it before. Never thought of Lincolnshire as a place she might return, or her sisters and their families and her mother as pieces with which she might fit again.

Or Jack, and his mother and sisters. The land, the hives, the bees.

She had so much to tell the bees. And there was so much forgiveness to beg.

"I shall see my mother and sisters," Marianne said unsteadily. "And Mr. Grahame, if he'll have me."

"A woman can never have too many sisters," said Mrs. Brodie. "You won't forget, I hope, how many you have here."

After suggesting a time for Marianne's departure the next day, the headmistress bade her good night. When she took her lamp and closed the door, the little room still seemed bright. It only needed Marianne's own lamp.

She sat on the bed, stroking the plain quilt that covered it, and looked around the simple room. She'd never made this space a home, saying the kitchen was her home. But her heart was divided. Maybe some part of her had always known she would leave again.

Without realizing it at the time, she'd always called Lincolnshire home. And she loved the idea of going toward it, not escaping. She could return home proud of what she'd learned. She knew a useful trade; she knew how to fight. She had sisters of the heart and, thank God, a home. Maybe someday she'd be able to be proud of how she mended the relationships she'd hurt.

All she could do was try.

For now, there was one more thing to do before sleep. She hung her apron on its hook, then pulled her book of recipes from the pocket. It was small in her hand, but represented much. Lessons learned, failures, successes. Experience documented, ignorance corrected.

She didn't need it anymore. She remembered it all.

Hefting the little book one more time, she set it on the washstand. A little something to help Sally, maybe. Something to show that Marianne had been here and that she'd made something new of herself.

Mrs. Brodie's Academy had been a good place to be, and she could come back someday if she wanted to. Because people left, and they returned. And it was all right.

If she was at peace in her own heart, and with those she loved, then it was all right.

## Chapter Nine

An unexpected frost had fallen during the night, and Jack had been awake since before dawn, trying to ward off damage. The great fields of wheat, oilseed, and barley would be all right, but delicate peas and beans would suffer, as would every kitchen garden from that of Westerby Grange to the humblest cottage.

Buckets in hand, Jack and every servant and tenant he could rouse had paced the rows, dribbling water onto each growing thing to thaw it before sunrise. It was grueling and arduous, this race against the sun and the sudden snap of cold.

By the time day broke, they had saved almost everything. Viola and the household staff of the Grange saw a hearty breakfast served in the great entrance hall to everyone who had worked at the land that morning.

When the platters of eggs and rashers of bacon and thick, steaming oatcakes had all been consumed, the other men melted off to the usual day's work.

"And where are you off to?" Viola, pin-neat in a lavender morning dress, asked Jack. "No one would fault you for finding your bed again."

True, though he didn't feel like sleep. The success of the night's task had buoyed him, depending as it did on the speed and purpose of his own work.

"While I'm dirty anyway," he decided, "I'll spend some time working on the old Redfern stable."

Viola examined the delicate lace at her sleeves. "Better you than me. In a few hours, I'll send someone to you with water and something to eat, if you like."

"Thanks, Vee." Pecking her on the cheek and laughing at her grimace and protest against his dirt, Jack left the house. He tramped across the Grahame lands, crossing onto those that had once belonged to the Redferns.

They had all altered, thanks to Helena's money. Croplands no longer flooded due to poor drainage; the fields had been replanted with more profitable grains. Tenants had been recruited and secured, and Jack's father's purchase of the Redfern lands from Marianne's widowed mother had added hundreds of acres. The house had been sold separately, along with a bit of land, to rich Londoners who wanted a bucolic country home but didn't care to farm.

Jack avoided the sight of it, the house where Marianne had grown up. He'd already enough reminders of Marianne tucked within his own brain. By cutting across the land to the east of it, he arrived at his destination.

The old stable hadn't been used for its intended purpose since Jack's childhood. It was slope-floored and dim, an Elizabethan relic that had been replaced with a modern construction much nearer the house. This stable was off by itself in a pasture. The remains of a footpath and training track indicated that it might once have been part of a stud facility. For decades, it had been nothing but a catch place for things that weren't quite good enough to use but not quite bad enough to discard.

The day after Jack's arrival, he'd oiled the rusty old lock and wrestled it open, then shoved back one of the great doors and eyed the space. It had been well built of the same red brick as the grand homes hereabouts, roofed in slate that had kept the place sound—or nearly so. Here and there, broken slates had allowed water to damage the roof structure, to trickle in and turn tools into heaps of mildew and rust. An out-of-favor carriage had become a nest for mice, the stuffing of its squabs tugged and pulled in clouds of horsehair and batting. And the condition of the tack left behind was not worth speaking of.

But the way it was wasn't the way it would always have to be. And in the three days since Jack had arrived, he'd drawn up rough plans for the way the building could be changed. He'd brought over new slates and stowed them in the stable, and today he'd begin to repair the roof.

He retrieved a ladder from the stable, relieved that it was decently sound, and hefted a roll of heavy wool batting onto his back. Slates were fragile, strong though they were once in place, and he'd need to protect them from his own weight.

With a few slates at a time, he climbed the ladder, gingerly moved across the roof on the roll of batting to the necessary spot, then removed the broken shingle and put the new piece of drilled stone in its place. Driving it in with long copper nails, he moved on to the next, and the next.

The frost was gone from the air, though the day remained cool. Jack was grateful for a breeze as he worked at the stable roof. The new slates were far darker than the old, which had been paled by decades of rain and sun—or maybe just purchased from a different quarry. Jack's work stood out from the rest of the roof like freckles on a face. He rather liked it, seeing the progress he'd made. Sometimes it was nice to be reminded that he'd done something with his time.

Just as Marianne did, meal after meal, bringing contented bellies to students and teachers and servants. Marianne, making a good wage all those years, safe and capable because someone had taken her in and taught her what she needed to know.

He'd do the same, however he could. And this was where he'd do it.

"You're humming," called up a voice from below. Startled, he dropped his hammer, cracking the slate he'd been about to install.

And he realized he *had* been humming.

And that Marianne Redfern was no longer in London, but standing on the ground looking up at him. Smiling.

His heart, thumping from the surprise of her voice, picked up yet more speed. It was the work of a minute to scramble back to the ladder—carefully, of course, on the batting—and slide down. "Marianne," he said as soon as his feet touched the earth. "Marianne," he said again, taking a step toward her. "You're—what are you doing here? How did you get here?"

She shaded her eyes with the flat of her hand, squinting at him. "I came home. Mrs. Brodie gave me the use of her private carriage."

Surely he was imagining all of this. Viola hadn't sent him any food or water yet, and he was imagining things. "Her private carriage. The use of it. For a journey of more than one hundred miles."

"Well, yes. She said she wouldn't feel right about me traveling alone on a stage or the mail."

Jack shook his head. "What kind of academy *is* this?"

"It's an exceptional one." Marianne grinned.

"Yes, I think it is." He looked at the stack of remaining slates on the ground. The roof, with so much done and so much left to do. "And you're here…why?"

Her expression went serious. Her hand fell to her side, and she looked at Jack with frank eyes under straight brows. "I came to apologize to you."

He started to sit on the slates, then thought better of it and sank to the ground. "Forgive me," he said. "It's already been a long day. I just—could you say that again?"

"That I came to apologize to you?" She sat on the ground beside him, careless of her familiar old work dress. "I did. And I do forgive you, just as you asked."

He poked her in the arm. "Oh, good. You're real."

She poked him back. "I'm real. I'm really here. And I wanted to see you. I missed you, after all the days I'd seen you in London. I decided I didn't want to get used to missing you again. Jack, I was so proud and superior. I shouldn't have—"

"You shouldn't have had to go to the slightest bit of trouble." Oh, she would break him to bits with her apology. She would make him anew. "Why I didn't fall on my knees and beg for your hand at once, I don't know."

"Because we couldn't bear that the past meant nothing." She smiled. "And because you were holding all those strawberries. If you knelt, you might have dropped them."

"Then you do forgive me? For giving you up?"

It was all he'd wanted—and when she shook her head, cold dismay washed over him.

Until she replied. "But you didn't, did you? At least, you didn't give up on me. And so there is nothing for me to forgive. If we'd wed eight years ago, we wouldn't be here together like this. I couldn't have surprised you today when you were all dirty and strong and capable. And today…"

She blushed. He smiled, the dismay ebbing like a wave, only to be replaced by peace. "Today is beautiful," he said. Heedless of the dirt beneath his nails, the slate dust and detritus that covered him, he took her hand in his.

They sat a moment in silence. Marianne tipped her head back, letting the breeze stroke her cheeks. "I haven't been on this land for years. I'm glad to see it again."

"It missed you," he said, not quite saying what he meant.

She turned her face to Jack's, imploring. "Can you forgive me for my pride and anger? I asked you to go because I thought you didn't trust me."

"What a pair we've been. I left because I thought you didn't trust me." He squeezed her hand. "I'm not sure I trusted myself—to do the right thing, I mean. But I've since decided if I'm making choices that are motivated by love, then…that's the best I can do."

"And you left because you love me."

He'd never seen anything as beautiful as her green eyes, looking into his with such depth and sweetness. "I do. I wanted to please you as best I could, Marianne. Even if that meant removing myself from your presence."

"I missed you so much. I chased you away when you meant to help, and—once you were gone, the cooking lost its savor."

Her lips twitched. He groaned. "You shouldn't make terrible puns when you're telling me nice things. You've told me that I love you, which is quite correct. Won't you tell me what you feel?"

"I want to be with you, Jack. Even if that means removing myself from London." She smiled. "Though it's not really leaving London; it's coming back home. They ought to be the same thing, but somehow they're not."

He seized on the meaning behind the words. "So you love me."

"As you say," she said. "I love you."

"Well. That's settled." Relief, gladness, peace were warm like the sun overhead, cool like the wind that softened its heat. They were balanced. Everything balanced. "And we're to spend our whole lives forgiving each other, are we?"

Marianne raised a brow. "I should hope so. The alternatives are being perfect—"

"Impossible," he sighed.

"—or not being together, or not forgiving each other."

"Intolerable," he said. "I see. You're quite right, we should forgive each other thoroughly and frequently."

"Something in the tone of your voice is…hmm. Do you mean 'forgive,' or do you mean something more…" She trailed off.

"Yes," he said.

Again, she blushed, and he smiled. "So you left your kitchen." He still had a difficult time believing it.

"It's not mine; it's the academy's. And I can cook and create and show caring wherever I am. I should be sad to think I could only do that in one place. I'll sort it out somehow."

She freed her hand from his, unfolding to her feet to look at his work. "But what are you doing? Repairing my father's old stable? This hasn't been used since I was a child."

"Ah. You inspired it. Or maybe your academy did." Standing beside her, he pointed up at what he'd done. Explained what there was left to do. Once the space within was cleared, the old stalls demolished, there would be a great open space for whatever one wished. It would be a simple matter to install ovens and worktables—though one needn't limit oneself.

"If I can't find a cook to teach lessons here, I'll still be able to use it. Think of the ballroom at Mrs. Brodie's Academy, used for far more than dancing." Reflexively, he rubbed his shoulder at the memory. "Why, in a space like this, anything could be taught."

Marianne had listened thoughtfully, nodding her understanding. Now she looked into the open door of the stable, reared back, and returned to Jack. "It's a disaster in there."

"It's not ready for a teacher yet, no," he agreed.

"So." She looked coyly at him, gaze aslant. "You haven't anyone in mind for the job, you said?"

"I always have you in mind. But I wasn't going to ask anything more of you, certainly not to leave London for me."

"But I didn't leave London. I came home." She beamed at him, and he felt like a king. "This is brilliant. It'll be like your own academy. You'll be helping girls take care of themselves, just as Mrs. Brodie did."

"Just as you've done all these years," he added. "Look, I want to be scrupulously honest with you. Every fruit has a stone in it, and this building is the stone. I don't want to tell you that it will take a great deal of time and money to bring back, but I'm telling you now all the same. I wish it would be easy for you to stay, no barriers in the way of the decision."

"You're here. My mother's here. Home is here. And a place to cook is here." She took his face between her palms and kissed him, sweet and lasting. "It's easy for me to stay. And sometimes one of us might need to leave, and that's all right. Just be honest with me."

"And if I leave, kiss you when I come back?"

"That is a requirement," she said. "Not every fruit has a stone, Jack. Some have seeds. When the fruit gets cut or damaged, that's when the seed can grow into something big and wonderful."

And it did. It had. It would. The friend of childhood would be the companion of adulthood and the strength of old age and the lover of a lifetime.

"Then you'll marry me?" Jack asked.

"As soon as the banns are called for us." Marianne took his hand again, looking at him with her heart in her eyes. "Come, let's tell the bees there's going to be a wedding."

Jack kissed her, and agreed, and went with her.

## Epilogue

*One year later*

"Use your favorite poem or song to help you keep a rhythm," Marianne told her new students. The girls looked at her like owls, eyes wide and blinking, half worried and half hopeful. "Get your hands into the dough—yes, just like that, Jemma. You can't hurt it, Elsie—it's all right even to slap it against the table."

From her table at the front of the large converted room, she showed the half-dozen students how to knead and pummel and otherwise abuse their bread dough. "If there's a fellow you're angry with, you can imagine his face," she said, working her fists into the soft mass.

As she hoped they would, the girls laughed, and they began to settle into a rhythm of their own at their long worktables. Some chanted in a quiet voice; some merely moved their lips. Some caught on quickly; some called for help from Mrs. Grahame—that was her!—and needed Marianne to stand near, coaching each step.

Marianne's dowry, invested in the funds, yielded a steady dividend, and she used it to pay the students a wage to attend her school of cookery. These girls needn't become maids at the age of twelve. They could learn to work with food, to gain themselves better posts. To help themselves and their families and those who loved them, lifelong.

With Marianne, they learned for a few hours each day, five days a week. Boys came for lessons at other times, other days. Some learned joinery, some studied languages and penmanship to prepare for clerkships. They too received a wage and were taught by those with knowledge.

Marianne still kneaded her dough to Shakespeare, but no longer to the words of *Macbeth*. Sometimes now it was *The Merchant of Venice*:

*The qual-i-ty of mer-cy is not strained.*
*It drop-peth as the gen-tle rain from heav'n.*

And sometimes she paced herself with sonnets. She particularly liked the one about the marriage of two minds, and love not altering when it alteration found.

Mercy and love, and the changes that time brought to a loved one. With these sweet balms, she had healed her heart. And whole, it was hers to give again.

She'd been like these girls once, uncertain of her place, though she'd had advantages they didn't all have. She'd had a home to leave and to return to and the knowledge of love, though she'd thought it dust and shaken it from her feet.

And she'd been hired by Mrs. Brodie, been taught by Mrs. Patchett, aided by Katie and Sally and the four Js and several other marvelous maids and assistants. They'd all seen to her future. Now she did her piece to see to the future of other girls, one roll and sauce and tart at a time. One perfectly cleaved apricot.

One strawberry in season, and one honeycomb still sticky sweet.

Outside, one of the last cool days of spring chilled the ground and the air; within the just-christened Helena Wilcox Grahame Academy, all was warm and bright. Marianne would finish today's lessons, then speak to Edith James about beginning to teach one day per week. The newest Grahame, Marianne and Jack's first child, would be born near Midsummer. While Marianne recovered from her confinement, she'd need someone to teach for her all the time.

Edith had been Marianne's first student, a quick and eager learner. She could take over the instruction, and well. And someday, so could several of the others. Love was generous, not selfish, and these girls watched out for each other.

They were exceptional young ladies, and sooner than they expected, they would be equal to anything.

## About Theresa Romain

Theresa Romain is the bestselling author of historical romances, including the Matchmaker trilogy, the Holiday Pleasures series, the Royal Rewards series, and the Romance of the Turf trilogy. Praised as "one of the rising stars of Regency historical romance" (*Booklist*), she has received starred reviews from Booklist and was a 2016 RITA® finalist. A member of Romance Writers of America and its Regency specialty chapter The Beau Monde, Theresa is hard at work on her next novel from her home in the Midwest.

To keep up with all the news about Theresa's upcoming books, please visit theresaromain.com and sign up for her newsletter.

## Books by Theresa Romain

If you enjoyed this story, read more from Theresa:

**The Romance of the Turf** series—featuring a talented but troubled family at the heart of the Regency horse-racing world.

**The Royal Rewards** series—in which a theft from the Royal Mint leads to treasure hunts, heists, and HEAs.

**The Matchmaker Trilogy**—characters at the fringes of the ton find love in these Regency twists on classic literature.

**The Holiday Pleasures** series—festive romances featuring connected characters.

More information about all her series, including trivia and excerpts, can be found at theresaromain.com/books/.

*Counterfeit Scandal*

*A Novella*

*Shana Galen*

## Chapter One

Bridget Lavery moved among her students, observing their penmanship. It was her last class of the day and comprised of about twelve girls ages eight to ten. Officially, she taught art, reading, and penmanship.

Unofficially, she taught counterfeiting.

What was counterfeiting currency but the melding of art and penmanship? These pupils were too young to try their hand at actual counterfeiting, but they were learning to copy the styles of writing on various bank notes issued by England, as well as other countries.

"That's very good, Susan," she said as she peered over the shoulder of a thin blond girl. Most of the work in this class looked rough and unrefined, but Susan's hand was exceptionally steady, and she had a good eye for her age.

"Thank you, Mrs. Lavery," Susan said, smiling up at her. The little girl had blue eyes, and whenever Bridget looked into them, her chest tightened. Susan's eyes were almost the same blue as James's. He would be the same age as the youngest girls in the room too. Just eight.

When Bridget looked at Susan's blond hair, she wondered if James's hair was still blond, or whether it had turned darker like her own.

Bridget forced herself to keep moving, to continue nodding and smiling at the girls' work, but her mind was elsewhere, lost in memories of a smiling toddler, arms out as he wobbled toward her on unsteady legs.

"Mrs. Lavery?"

Bridget blinked and glanced quickly at Abigail, whose hand was raised. "It's past four o'clock. May we be dismissed?"

Bridget looked at the small clock on her desk. It was indeed almost five minutes past the hour. How careless of her! She had made the girls late to their pickpocketing class with Mrs. Chalmers.

"Of course. I am so sorry. Gather your materials, and we will continue with this practice next time we meet."

Efficient as always, the girls were filing out the door within moments, a sea of blue in their school dresses. As soon as the last girl filed out, Bridget gathered her personal items and rushed to follow. This was the worst possible day to be caught daydreaming. She had an appointment at half past four near Covent Garden, and she did not want to be late. She stopped by the room she shared with

Mademoiselle Valérie Gagne—who taught French and accent modification—pulled on gloves and a hat, and rushed down the stairs, past a ballroom filled with older girls practicing sharp kicks to hay targets, and out the front door.

A few minutes later, she was jostling among the crowds on Piccadilly, wary of pickpockets, ignoring the cries of hawkers, and trying to stay clear of carriages with overzealous drivers. The boarding house was farther than she would have liked, but she couldn't afford any of the rooms in Marylebone. She'd investigated every vacancy. She located the street she sought, turned right, and slowed. The street was not as busy as many of the others and not at all what she would call safe. People sat in doorways and watched her pass. As she was dressed little better than they, though her clothes were cleaner, they mostly ignored her.

Bridget carried a knife in her pocket just in case. She'd never had to use it. On occasion, she'd had to pull it out, whereby the lad—almost always a young boy or boys—accosting her decided she wasn't worth the trouble. Usually, she never brought blunt with her when walking alone. Today, she had a shilling tucked in her glove. The rest of her savings was safely hidden back at Mrs. Brodie's Academy. Bridget doubted even Valérie could have found it, not that Valérie would ever steal from her.

But Bridget didn't trust anyone.

Yesterday, when Valérie had been teaching and Bridget had an hour's break, she'd locked their door, pried up the floorboard, taken the money out, and counted it. She had twelve shillings and six pence saved. It wasn't much, considering, but she hoped it would be enough to rent a small room in a boarding house. Once she had a room, she could claim James again—if she could find him.

She studied the numbers printed on the buildings until she found the one she sought. A Mrs. Jacobs had advertised "clean, furnished rooms at affordable prices."

Bridget tapped on the door and waited until a woman with messy brown hair and a dirty apron pulled it open. "What do you want?"

"I'm looking for Mrs. Jacobs. I sent a note inquiring about the room for rent and was told to come at half past four."

The woman's eyes slid down Bridget and back up again. "And who are you?"

"Bridget Lavery. Are you Mrs. Jacobs?"

"I am. Do you have a husband?" Mrs. Jacob's eyes narrowed. "I'm not running a bawdy house."

Bridget felt her cheeks color. "My husband is dead. I teach at Mrs. Brodie's Academy in Manchester Square. You may speak to Mrs. Brodie if you'd like a reference or proof I'm not a harlot."

Bridget hoped the headmistress was in London at the moment. She often traveled, and she hadn't seen her for a few days.

Mrs. Jacobs opened the door wider, nodding. "The school don't give you a room?"

"It does, but I have a young son, and the academy is for young ladies. If I want him to live with me, I must procure my own lodging."

The door inched closed again. "Boys can be trouble."

"This one won't be."

The two women eyed each other for a long moment, and then Mrs. Jacobs stepped back. "Come in, Mrs. Lavery. I'll show you the room."

Mrs. Jacobs led her through a dark common room and up a staircase with worn carpet. The subtle scent of mold and cooked onions lingered in the air. At the landing, Mrs. Jacobs continued to the second floor. Bridget frowned. She had been hoping for a room on the first floor, as the top floor would be hot in summer and cold in winter.

"The men's rooms are on the first floor," Mrs. Jacobs said, as though reading her mind. "The women are up here."

The second floor was dark, and Bridget squinted as Mrs. Jacobs led her to the end of the corridor, pulled out a large keyring, selected a key, and opened the door.

She motioned Bridget inside, and Bridget walked in cautiously. The room was small and dingy. It had a bed, a table with one chair, and a basin with a pitcher. "I thought the advertisement said the room was furnished."

"This is furnished," Mrs. Jacobs countered. "What more do you need?" She blew out a breath. "You even have curtains on the windows. Sewed them myself."

Bridget crossed to the window at the other end of the room, all of six steps, and opened the curtains. The window looked out on another building and down into an alleyway. She closed the curtains again.

"How much?"

"One shilling and two pence a week."

It was reasonable, though she'd hoped for better. "Is coal included?"

"That's extra."

"What about meals?"

"Extra."

She could take meals at the school, but James needed to eat. "Water?"

"There's a well in the yard. Help yourself."

"I'll give you a shilling a week for it."

"It's a shilling and two pence, and I won't take less." Mrs. Jacobs folded her arms over her chest with finality. Bridget would not be deterred, however. For almost two years, she had been working toward the goal of reclaiming James. She had a plan, and obtaining a room was the last step before she sought James. She needed this room, dingy as it was.

"I'll pay a shilling and two pence if that price includes a pail of coal a week."

Mrs. Jacobs hesitated, then began to shake her head.

"I will give you one shilling now."

The landlady considered. She could continue to haggle, but then she risked the chance of having the room remain vacant. No tenant meant no blunt. She held out her hand. "I'll agree, provided that Mrs. Brodie vouches for you."

Bridget nodded, removed her glove, and placed the shilling in Mrs. Jacobs's palm. It was gone in an instant.

"I'll speak to Mrs. Brodie first thing in the morning. If she says you're a good girl, you and the boy can move in tomorrow evening."

"Very good. It will just be me for now."

"Why is that? Where is the boy living?"

"It will take me time to send for him," she said, keeping her answer vague.

Mrs. Jacobs nodded. "As long as he doesn't cause trouble."

"He won't." Of course, she couldn't know that. She hadn't seen James since he was barely three. She didn't know what sort of boy he'd grown into in the intervening years. And yet, she was well-versed in dealing with unruly children. She could handle her own son, and she would.

She just had to find him first. She'd gone to the orphanage where she'd left James before she'd been sent to Fleet Prison with Robbie, but the St. Dismas Home for Wayward Youth had burned down, and no one seemed to know what had happened to the boys who'd lived there.

She hadn't known how to go about discovering more. She considered hiring an investigator to look into the matter, but she feared the expense would be too dear.

Mrs. Jacobs, evidently convinced she'd shown the new tenant enough of the room, motioned her out and locked the door again. She began what sounded like a well-rehearsed speech about meals and noise and visitors as she led Bridget back down the stairs. Bridget made sounds of assent, but she was looking at the cracked paint on the walls and wondering what James would think of their new home. What would he think of her? Could he ever forgive her for abandoning him?

Finally at the front door, the two ladies said their goodbyes, and Mrs. Jacobs opened the door for Bridget just as a man was opening it from the outside.

"Pardon me, ladies," he said when he saw that he had blocked their way.

Bridget began to say something along the lines of, *It is nothing, sir*, but then she looked up and into his face.

Those eyes. She knew of only two people in the world with that exact shade of blue. One was James and the other his father.

Caleb Harris felt his smile fade. There had only ever been a few times in his life where he hadn't known what to do. Seeing her again was one of those rare times. He'd known it might happen when he was sent back to England and then to London. He'd prepared several speeches in the unlikely event that he saw her.

But looking at her now, her golden-brown eyes riveted to his face, her expression like that of a person who had seen a ghost, he couldn't think of a single word.

They stared at each other for what seemed like hours, though it was probably only a few seconds. It was long enough for Mrs. Jacobs to clear her throat conspicuously. "Do you two know each other?"

"Yes," he said at the same time that she said, "No."

Mrs. Jacobs looked from one to the other.

He was a bloody idiot. Why had he said *yes*? At least Bridget still had her wits about her. "I misspoke." Caleb removed his hat politely. "I'm afraid I have not had the pleasure of making this lady's acquaintance."

"Mrs. Lavery, this is Mr. Smith. Mr. Smith, Mrs. Lavery."

He nodded. "A pleasure, Mrs. Lavery." She hadn't been Bridget Lavery when he'd known her. Nor had she been married. Of course, he hadn't been Smith back then either.

"Mr. Smith." She nodded right back. He'd thought it impossible for her warm, golden eyes to ever look icy, but she managed it now. "If you'll excuse me."

He stepped quickly aside as she moved toward the door. Once in the doorway, she turned back to Mrs. Jacobs. "Thank you, madam. I will see you tomorrow."

So she was returning? Could she be renting a room here? He watched as she walked away until that view was obscured when Mrs. Jacobs closed the door. The landlady turned to him, but before she could speak, he started for the stairs. "Excuse me, Mrs. Jacobs. No time to talk now."

He took the steps two at a time, withdrew his key from his pocket, and had it ready at the door to his room. Once inside, he leaped over the traps he'd laid and made straight for the window. He pulled the curtains apart and looked out on the street. She was there, just now at the end of the lane. He could still catch her.

He yanked the window up, put one leg over, grasped a clothesline, and swung out. One hand on the clothesline, he reached for the drainpipe with the other, then shimmied down and ran to catch up with Bridget.

He shouldered past people, earning a few deserved curses, until he caught sight of her plain blue dress and white bonnet in the crowd. With a last burst of speed, he caught up to her, matching his pace to hers and walking beside her.

She looked over at him as though seeing him beside her, out of breath and hatless, did not surprise her at all.

"I thought you were dead," she said.

"That was what everyone was made to think. It was the only way to ensure my survival across enemy lines."

"The Foreign Office." Her voice held enough contempt to fill a sea. "I should have known they lied. I expect that of them." She glanced at him, her eyes still cold. "I didn't expect it of you."

"I couldn't tell you." He had to twist sideways to avoid bumping into two men walking side by side. "I couldn't tell anyone.

I didn't even know I'd been reassigned until the day before I was to leave."

"So you did have time to tell me."

"I was ordered to tell no one."

She stopped so suddenly that he walked on for two or three steps before he realized she wasn't beside him. He turned and walked back to her.

"And what are your orders now, Mr. *Smith?* Surely not to speak to me."

She wasn't wrong. The last thing he should have been doing at the moment was speaking to anyone who had known him before. Unless he had a death wish. Which he didn't.

She nodded with understanding. "Well, then you had better not be seen with me, and since I am moving into Mrs. Jacobs's boarding house and have already paid a shilling I can ill afford to lose for the privilege, you had better move out."

"Bridget—"

"Mrs. Lavery. You're not the only one with a different name."

"I'm sorry I missed the wedding."

"You missed much more than that. Good day, Mr. Smith."

She turned and marched away, leaving him wondering and wishing things might have been different.

## Chapter Two

Bridget was famished, but she didn't go down to dinner at six. Mrs. White was the new cook, and her offerings were still somewhat unpredictable. Bridget still missed Mrs. Redfern's colcannon, but she did not think she could have kept even soda bread down at the moment. Her thoughts were in turmoil, and her heart hadn't stopped pounding since she'd seen him.

Caleb wasn't dead. Some part of her had always hoped that was true. She'd known he was an agent for the Foreign Office, known he might be sent to the Continent on a dangerous mission, but she had never believed he would lie to her. He might lie to everyone else, but she'd trusted he would tell her the truth.

She'd thought he loved her.

Foolish girl.

She'd removed her dress and her shoes and stockings and lay on her bed in her stays and chemise. She was staring at the pattern of plaster on the ceiling when she heard Valérie's shoes on the wood outside the door. She didn't look up when Valérie entered.

"Are you ill?" her roommate asked, her voice tinged with the slight lilt of French.

"No, I'm…" She didn't know what she was.

Valérie closed the door behind her and took a seat on the edge of her bed, just across from Bridget's. "Then why did you not come down to dinner? Did something happen? Had Mrs. Jacobs already rented the room?"

"No. I rented the room, assuming Mrs. Brodie gives me a good recommendation."

"She will. Of course." Valérie cocked her head, her dark curls spilling over her shoulder. She was young and pretty and could have easily found a husband. But she had her reasons for working at the academy—just as Bridget did.

"Then what has upset you, Bridget?"

"I saw Caleb at the boarding house."

"Caleb?" She frowned, then her dark eyes widened. "Not *the* Caleb. Not the father of your son?"

"Yes. That Caleb." The image of him flashed in her mind. He still had that curly brown hair she'd loved to run her hands through and a lean face with a square jaw. He'd been dressed in a dark coat and trousers that didn't fit him nearly as well as his clothing had in the past, but she suspected he'd chosen to be inconspicuous rather than fashionable.

And then there were the eyes.

Valérie rose. "But this is good news, no? You thought he was dead, and he is alive!"

Bridget gave her a long look from under lowered lashes. "It's not good news, Val, because it means that he lied to me. He knew he would be sent to the Continent and we would be told he was dead, and he let me believe that along with everyone else."

"Surely he had no choice."

Bridget sat up. "One always has a choice."

"This is true enough, but what would you have done differently if he had told you of the plan? You did not know you were with child when he left. What choice did you have but to marry?"

"I might have gone to the men at the upper levels of the Foreign Office and demanded they contact him."

Valérie made a *pfft* sound. "You know they would have perpetuated their lie. You worked for them long enough to understand that."

She shrugged. "Perhaps I wouldn't have done anything differently then, but it doesn't change the fact that Caleb lied to me. He let me believe he was dead. I thought—well, you know what I thought. He obviously didn't love me."

"I think only he can answer that. Did you tell him about his son?"

"No! I have no reason to. I don't know where James is, and I doubt I'll ever see Caleb again. I told him he had to move out of the boarding house."

Valérie laughed. "But of course you did! Will he listen?"

"He's using another name now, and I doubt he wants to be associated with his former acquaintances. I think he'll be gone before I move in tomorrow night."

Valérie's eyes widened. "Tomorrow night? So soon? What will I do without you?"

"Spread all of your clothing out and sing at the top of your lungs every morning?"

"Nonsense. I will miss your grumpy face in the mornings."

"You can see it before the first class period, and I don't hear you complaining about the extra space."

"My dresses are rather crushed."

Suddenly, Bridget threw her arms around Valérie. "I'll miss you too."

Valérie hugged her back. "I never thought I would hear you say such words. You were adamant you did not want a roommate."

"After three years in debtor's prison, you would want privacy too."

"I hope I gave you that."

"You did, and you gave me something more important."

Valérie raised a brow.

"Friendship."

The next morning, Bridget stood before a class of older girls, ages sixteen to eighteen. Most of them had been at the academy for several years and had mastered the skills taught—both conventional and unconventional. A few had become truly exceptional. As she surveyed them, Bridget had every confidence they would go out into the world and succeed. They could defend themselves and had all the skills ladies did and a few more besides.

"I don't need to remind you that forgery is a hanging offense," Bridget was saying. "You should not use the skill without weighing the consequences of being caught. Eleanor, would you use the skill to pay a debt?"

Eleanor, whose dark blond hair always seemed to escape her cap, considered. "I think it would depend on the amount, Mrs. Lavery. For a small debt, no. For a larger one, it might be worthwhile to avoid debtor's prison."

If these girls thought debtor's prison was the worst that could happen to them, perhaps she had been hasty in her earlier judgment of their readiness.

"You think death is preferable to debtor's prison?"

Eleanor looked down. "I'm not certain."

Beth, one of Eleanor's friends, raised her hand and spoke when Bridget nodded at her. "When would you counterfeit money, Mrs. Lavery? How did you gain the skills?"

She supposed it was time she told them. Many of them were leaving the academy soon, and the others were old enough to know. "My father taught me," she said. A few of the girls, those from more sheltered homes, raised their brows. "He was caught by the government and was offered a choice between hanging or working for the Foreign Office. He chose the Foreign Office and was instrumental in devising the plan to counterfeit Continental currency, which undermined the economy and the war efforts of the newly formed United States of America.

"Early in the war against Napoleon, I was recruited by the Foreign Office to do much the same thing for France and its allies. So you see, there are reasons to counterfeit currency."

Mary, one of the older girls, raised her hand. "Are there any reasons we might risk a charge of treason to counterfeit currency, Miss Lavery?"

"Good question, Mary. Yes. You might find yourself in a situation where your life is at risk and you must flee quickly, but you lack the funds to pay for transport. That might be a situation in which it would be worth risking the creation of counterfeit currency."

"But not to stay out of debtor's prison?" Eleanor asked.

Bridget shrugged. "If you are responsible for the debt, then it hardly seems fair to make others pay for your carelessness. And when you give a tradesman a counterfeit bill, he is the one who loses pay for honest work."

That had certainly been her way of thinking when she and Robbie had found themselves in the position of being sent to debtor's prison. Robbie had suggested she counterfeit the money necessary to free them from their debt, and Bridget had argued his plan was madness. Not only would the tradesmen easily find them out and report them, but much of his debt was to the banks themselves. Bankers were notorious for spotting forgeries, even those as good as Bridget's.

She'd been angry at Robbie for years for borrowing money for foolish schemes that had not worked out. In the end, though, when he lay dying in Fleet Prison, she couldn't be angry. He had suffered more than he deserved for his sins. She couldn't regret choosing not to counterfeit the currency, though. If she had, they would both be dead, and James really would be an orphan.

Now, Bridget reached into her drawer and withdrew a few notes of authentic Continental currency her father had collected. She passed them out, two girls sharing one note, as well as some of the special paper the colonists had used to print the currency and which the British had intercepted. "For the rest of the class, practice creating counterfeit dollars. You'll see each state produced its own design, so if you finish before time is up, switch dollars with another pair of girls."

The girls put their heads down and began to work. In the meantime, Bridget went to the window and peered out. The day had dawned cloudy and cool for June. The clouds hung low, promising rain. She hoped that it rained sooner rather than later, as she would have to move her personal items to Mrs. Jacobs's boarding house tonight, and she did not relish arriving looking like a wet sewer rat.

Not that it mattered, as Caleb would have gone by now. She'd told him to leave, and he was enough of a gentleman to adhere to her wishes. It wasn't as though he wanted to see her at any rate. For a man with his talents, it would have been easy to track her down when he returned to London. He'd made no effort to do so.

She was better off without him, and she'd waste no more time thinking of him. She had bigger problems—the first of these being how to find James. She'd asked Mrs. Brodie for a recommendation of an investigator who might help with her search, and the lady had provided her with a name. Now, as her pupils forged Continental dollars, Bridget sat at her desk and wrote a short message to the man requesting an interview.

Caleb didn't relocate. He had no great love for Mrs. Jacobs or her rooms, but he did find he cared a great deal for Bridget O'Brien—Bridget Lavery now. He hadn't forgotten her over all these years. He'd thought of her more often than he would have liked. He'd tried to forget her, told himself she had forgotten him, but though he'd found companionship with other women, he'd never found the sense of completeness he'd felt with Bridget.

She was angry at him. Of course, she was. She didn't understand that it hadn't been his decision to leave her or to perpetuate the myth that he was dead. He'd had no choice, or he would be dead in truth right now.

If he wasn't careful, he could still end up dead.

Caleb paced his small, dingy room in Mrs. Jacobs's boarding house and tried not to listen for the door. He did not think Bridget would arrive until later that evening, but he couldn't seem to concentrate on anything but her imminent arrival. Knowing she would soon be under the same roof as he was a distraction.

That was all the more reason for him to move. He'd done his work on the Continent too well, and now he had a price on his head. He'd been hiding all over the Continent for years, but the last time the Foreign Office had tried to relocate him, Caleb had insisted on coming home to London. He'd argued he could be lost in London as well as Lisbon or Madrid, and at least in London he'd be home.

They'd given him another name and a new set of papers and housed him in Covent Garden. He was withering away with boredom and obscurity. Every day, he thought it less and less likely that any assassins had tracked him to London or were looking for him there, but the government still advised caution. A man with a price on his head could not be too cautious.

And so Caleb sat in his room, day after day and night after night. He made an occasional trip out for an apple or whatever the hawkers were selling near the theater. Mrs. Jacobs's cook seemed to manage only boiled potatoes and bland soup. He'd been coming home from just such an excursion yesterday when he'd come face-to-face with Bridget.

He would have known her anywhere. She was still so beautiful that seeing her had all but taken his breath away. The passage of time had made her only more beautiful. He'd had a moment of jealousy when he realized she'd married. He'd pushed it aside, because he'd been no saint himself, but he did have hope when he'd noted her husband was not with her. Perhaps she'd done as so many other women—given herself the title of Mrs. without the actual husband to go with it.

He stopped at a sound, listening hard, but it was not the front door, only one of the men walking past his room on the way down the stairs.

Caleb knew he could not pick up where he'd left off with Bridget. For one, he was a danger to anyone who might get close to him. And there was the small matter of her hating him and telling him to move away so she would not have to be near him.

He would move. He couldn't behave like some lovesick poet, watching out windows and hoping for a glimpse of her. But it wasn't as easy as she seemed to think. He couldn't just leave. He had to inform the Foreign Office and wait for approval and a new location.

He'd explain all of this when—if—he saw her.

That opportunity came sooner than he'd thought and in a way he didn't expect. She knocked on his door.

Caleb had been in his room attempting to read. He hadn't been very successful, as he'd heard her arrive the evening before and had spent most of the night and all of the day wondering if she was in her room and what she might be doing.

His heart had leaped into his throat when he'd heard the knock, but he'd pushed it back down again. It couldn't be her. She wouldn't knock on his door. She wouldn't risk being seen on the men's floor immediately after moving in. Caleb had considered pretending he wasn't in, then rose and, knife in hand—one couldn't be too careful—opened the door a sliver.

Her golden-brown eyes peered at him from the thin slice of hallway between the wooden casement. Immediately, he flung the door open all the way, grabbed her arm, pulled her inside, then looked out to make sure no one had seen them.

The corridor was blissfully empty.

Caleb closed the door and locked it.

"That was rather dramatic," she said. He looked at her, then moved back a step, careful not to trip over the all but invisible wire of one of his traps. He need space as he didn't trust himself not to try to take her into his arms.

"Didn't Mrs. Jacobs explain the rules?" he asked.

"Yes, but I thought this worth the risk."

He folded his arms over his chest. "I know you asked me to vacate the house. It's not as easy as that, but I am—"

She waved a hand. "That's not what this is about. I'm actually glad you are still here."

There went his heart into his throat again. He swallowed. "Why is that?" His voice was slightly higher than he would have liked, but it didn't falter.

"Because I need your help."

Caleb took a breath and attempted to slow his racing heart. "Shouldn't you ask your husband for help?"

"I am asking you. I went to a man today with the intent of hiring him to find…a missing person. He agreed, but the price he asked was too high. I've searched for him myself but have exhausted my limited skills in this area. I know you have talents others do not. I thought you might do this for me as a favor." She looked down at the floor and then back up again. "Because it concerns you as well."

"How is that?"

"The person I am searching for is your son."

*Chapter Three*

Caleb reached for the table edge, his legs as unsteady as those of a man who'd just walked out of a gin house. "What did you say?"

"You'd better sit down. You've gone white as a sheet."

"Watch the wire," he said.

She looked down then up at the bucket of nails suspended above her. Stepping over the wire, she reached for one of the chairs at his table and pulled it out, then pushed him down onto it. She looked warily about his room. "Are there any other traps?"

"Not at the moment."

"This is bigger than my room, and your furnishings are not quite so worn."

He didn't have the wherewithal to tell her that he'd spent some of his all-too-ample time making the room comfortable and setting up traps.

"What does your window look out upon?"

At least she had the wits not to go to the curtains and fling them open. And she had the sense to know he'd had a big shock and that speaking of trivialities would mitigate the effect.

"The street."

"Of course. I look at another building and an alleyway." She bent to peer at him. "Do you need a drink, or have you recovered sufficiently?"

"You said I have a son?"

"Yes."

"I need a drink." He put a hand to his throat, which felt as though it had closed. He gestured to the floor by the washbasin where he kept a bottle of brandy. She crossed to it, and he had time to look at her. Yesterday, she'd been dressed plainly, almost matronly. Today, she wore a gown of deep red, practically an earthy brown. It was the sort of color that made her skin look flushed and healthy. Her hair was more elaborate as well. The severe bun had been replaced by a loose upsweep with a cascade of loose tendrils.

He might have taken a moment to admire her figure, but she set the brandy down hard on the table. "I can't find a glass."

"No need." He uncorked the neck and drank straight from the bottle, closing his eyes as the liquid burned a path down his throat. The warmth was immediate. He savored it, then took another healthy swig just for good measure.

"Better?" she asked.

"Yes. Do sit."

"I'd rather stand. I made a request for assistance."

"To find my son." He frowned. "How is it I have a son?"

Her brows went up. "I thought you, of all people, understood how these things work."

"We were—that is to say, *I* was careful." He hadn't spilled his seed inside her. He'd been careful to withdraw every time. He'd known he'd have to go to the Continent, and he'd known there was a good chance he would die. His plan had always been to find her and marry her if he survived. He hadn't known then that his work in the war would haunt him long afterward.

"I can only suppose that method of child prevention isn't infallible," she remarked dryly. "A few weeks after you left, I found I was with child."

Caleb drank again. This time, it was to prevent his legs from standing and carrying him toward her. He wanted to hold her. "I'm so sorry, Bridget." He raked a hand through his hair, regret slamming through him. "I can't imagine how awful that must have been for you. You must have known you'd be ostracized."

"I could have dealt with verbal abuse and slurs against my moral character if I had known you were coming back. If I thought you cared for me."

He did stand now. "Of course I cared for you. I told you." He reached for her, but she swatted his hand away.

"If you cared for me, you would have told me you were going, not have left it to the undersecretary to give me the news."

"Bridget." He spread his hands. "I couldn't tell you or anyone."

"And you were always one to follow the rules."

Caleb fisted a hand in his thoroughly disheveled hair. "This wasn't a rule. It was an order. If you only knew the nature of my mission, you would understand why it had to remain secret and why my death had to be fabricated."

"But I didn't understand any of that. I truly believed you were dead, and there I was, pregnant with your child."

"I didn't mean for that to happen. I meant to come back and marry you. I had no idea everything would go so wrong."

"Neither did I. Everything went very, very wrong, and I've spent the last six years trying to find a way to make it right."

Caleb pulled the other chair out from the table. "Please, sit. Tell me what happened."

Reluctantly, she sat, stiff and formal. He sat too and offered her the brandy bottle. She shook her head.

"Did you marry?" he asked. "Or was that a falsehood to protect your reputation?" He was an arse for asking this first. Of all the things he needed to know, this detail was probably the least important. But he wanted the answer. Was she another man's wife? Had he been the reason she'd married a man she didn't love, though he had to admit it would be better for all of them if she did love the man. What could Caleb offer her? And Bridget deserved happiness.

"I married a man named Robert Lavery."

Caleb furrowed his brow and drank again. He didn't remember any Lavery. "Did I know him?"

"No. After you went to the war and I realized I was pregnant, I left the Foreign Office. I found some work teaching art to students and sold a few of my own sketches to a printshop below my classroom. On my way coming and going, I met Robbie. He was kind, gentle, obviously infatuated with me."

Caleb had no doubt that it hadn't been difficult for her to attract men, even men willing to marry her. But the way she spoke of this Robbie made his hand on the brandy bottle loosen. She hadn't loved him. He should have wanted her to find love, but he couldn't bring himself to be that magnanimous. He supposed he was selfish that way.

"He asked me to marry him, and that's when I told him about the baby. He said he would love the baby like his own child. So I said yes. We married. I gave birth to James—"

"James. His name is James?"

She nodded. "I called him Jimmy sometimes because he was so little, and James seemed like such a big name for a little baby, but we named him James Lavery."

Caleb nodded, still trying to take it in. *He* had a son named James.

"Everything was good for a while," Bridget said.

Caleb sat straight. "And then what?"

"Robbie had debts. He had a bad habit of thinking there was a way to make easy money. He was always meeting men who had these wild ideas that Robbie was certain would pay off with a little investment."

Caleb closed his eyes.

"Some of the men were even legitimate businessmen. He went to the bank and signed papers, but of course, when the schemes didn't come to fruition, Robbie lost his money and then some."

"Did you make counterfeit currency?"

"I thought about it. When he realized how much he owed, he asked me to. But I said no. I knew we'd be caught eventually, especially if we paid the banks with counterfeits. I thought we'd find a way to get out of debtor's prison."

Caleb released the brandy bottle and clenched the table. He was too afraid he'd break the bottle if he continued to hold it.

Bridget in debtor's prison. Caleb would kill Lavery for that. How could he do that to his wife and child?

As if she knew what he was thinking, she said, "He died there."

"I'm sorry."

"No, you're not."

He wasn't.

"I knew how bad the prisons could be, and I didn't want James there with us. He was barely three. I also knew orphanages were awful, so I found one I thought was better than most of the others and left him there, promising to come back for him."

Now her dark eyes filled with tears. She didn't cry. She wouldn't allow that weakness, but her voice faltered for a long moment. "I wrote everyone I knew and asked for help. Robbie wrote everyone he knew. No one had enough to pay our debts."

"What about—"

"My Great-Aunt Fredricka? She didn't answer my letters, and I wrote her so many times. I knew she had the funds, and she sent me some anonymously, but she didn't approve of Robbie and wouldn't pay for him to leave prison—even if that meant I stayed in prison as well. And then he became ill. Almost everyone in Fleet Prison becomes ill at one point or another. Most of the time, we couldn't afford decent food or a bed or a fire. We starved and shivered and slept on the ground. Eventually, Robbie caught consumption. I don't know why I didn't get it. Sometimes, he was in so much pain, I wished it was me and not him. When he died, I wrote to Aunt Fredericka again, and she paid the debts within a week. I don't know how I can ever pay her back."

"I'm sure she doesn't care about that."

Bridget laughed. "Oh yes, she does. I have to send her a shilling a month until I've paid it all off. And when I asked why she didn't help me before Robbie died, she said because she knew if he went free, he'd just cast us into debt again."

"And now you're looking for..." He swallowed. "James. He'd be eight."

She nodded. "It took me a few months to find a position and then a year to save enough to afford a room of my own. I've been looking for him since I went free, but as near as I can figure, the orphanage burned in 1816. I assume it relocated, but no one seems to know where, and there are no orphanages called the St. Dismas Home for Wayward Boys in London."

"Where was it located?"

She told him the address in Spitalfields.

"You asked the shop owners nearby?"

"I did, but no one could help."

So she'd probably asked a few women. She couldn't exactly walk up to a man she didn't know in that area of Town and start a conversation, nor could she stroll into a tavern and ask questions over a pint of ale.

He could. He could do all that and more, but it would mean calling attention to himself. He was willing to risk it for Bridget and his son, if the risk was worth it.

"And what if he's been adopted? What if he's been made an apprentice or taken in by a couple unable to have children?"

She shook her head. "You know as well as I that's unlikely. But if he has, and he's happy, then I'd still like to see him, tell him I never forgot him, that I didn't abandon him."

And what would she tell the boy about his father? That he'd died in prison? The boy probably didn't know any other father but Lavery, and perhaps that was for the best. Caleb couldn't be any kind of father to him, not when he had to run and hide for his life.

"I'll help you," he said. "On one condition." Her gaze met his, and he cleared his throat. "When we find the boy, you don't tell him who I am."

Bridget agreed to Caleb's request and left his room. It was after ten in the evening and far too late to begin searching tonight. She had to be at the academy in the morning, but the day after was Saturday and she would have all day free.

She had to creep back to her room like some sort of criminal, but she couldn't afford to be caught on the men's floor her first night in the house. Mrs. Jacobs would throw her out with the rubbish.

She reached her room safely, closed and locked the door, then undressed for bed. Once under the covers, she lay awake staring at the ceiling. She could count on fingers and toes the number of times she'd had a room to herself. It seemed strange not to look over and see Valérie lying in her bed. Not to be able to whisper a few words and have an answer whispered back.

She'd always been the sort of person who fell asleep as soon as she lay down, but tonight, no matter which position she tried, she couldn't fall asleep. She knew it had to do with seeing Caleb again. He looked a bit older, a bit leaner, but little else about him had changed. When she spoke to him, sat with him, it was as though no time had passed since they'd seen each other. She was as comfortable with him as she'd always been.

She was as attracted to him as she'd always been too.

It had been difficult not to allow her eyes to stray to his bed and imagine him lying on it. Imagine herself lying there with him. It might have been nine years since they'd shared a bed, but she remembered what it was like to kiss him, as though they'd shared a kiss no more than a moment before.

His kisses were very much like the man himself—confident, easy, skilled.

Bridget remembered watching his hands roam over her body—first clothed and then in increasing stages of undress—and marveling at how he managed to make her feel so much with just the touch of a fingertip or the stroke of his thumb.

She couldn't blame him for her pregnancy. She'd been as willing as he to go to bed. And he had tried to prevent pregnancy. She'd never thought his method wouldn't work. It was only later, after making friends with several married women in prison, that she realized they'd been taking a risk every time they'd lain together. And they'd lain together quite a lot. She and Caleb hadn't been able to get enough of each other.

And then one day he'd been gone. He hadn't come into the Foreign Office, and when she'd gone to check on him at his lodgings, a man she didn't know opened the door. He said he didn't know Caleb and closed the door in her face. Her superiors at the Foreign Office admitted he'd been sent to the Continent, but that was all they would tell her. And then just a few days after she realized she was with child, Caleb's child, the undersecretary had come to her and told her Caleb had been killed.

Though she and Caleb had kept their relationship secret, the man seemed to know they were more than merely acquaintances. He'd taken one look at her face and sent her home for the day. The next day, she'd returned and handed in her resignation. They would have sent her away when they'd discovered her condition. She might have been able to keep a position as an art teacher longer. She'd had money saved. The Foreign Office paid well. It was ironic that she'd married to try to make her life easier and the marriage had ended up making it much, much harder. She might have faced scandal and contempt as a loose woman, but she would have been free. And she would have her son with her now.

Bridget turned over again and stared into the darkness of the room.

Caleb would find James. She knew he would, and maybe once she had her little boy in her arms again, it would be easier to forget the man who was his father.

The next day at the academy seemed to last an eternity. She was short-tempered with the little girls and demanding of the older. At the midday meal, she barely said a word, though Valérie tried on several occasions to encourage Bridget to speak more about her new room.

When Bridget was finally finished with classes, she didn't even wait to eat dinner—foolish, really, because the meal was included in her pay—and rushed back to Mrs. Jacobs's as quickly as she could. The residents there were eating as well, but since Bridget hadn't paid for food for the month, she didn't sit down with them. Instead, she walked slowly past the open door, hoping Caleb was inside. He was, and she caught his eye, then fled to her room.

She must have paced the small chamber thirty times before she heard footsteps coming down the corridor. Her heart leaped as it had all those years ago when they'd planned a rendezvous. But this time when she opened the door, she didn't jump into his arms. She'd told herself that part of their lives was over and done, but when she yanked the door open and saw him standing there, something happened when their eyes met. She felt the familiar fluttering in her belly and tightening in her chest. His eyes flashed with the sort of promise she'd always looked forward to.

"May I come in?" he asked. "It's not a good idea for me to be seen standing out here."

"Of course." She opened the door wide. She was an idiot. Standing there gaping at him. But he looked so handsome in his dark coat and breeches. His curly hair framed his square face and softened it.

He slid in, and she closed the door. Her small, empty room suddenly seemed even smaller. She squeezed past him and pulled out the chair at her table. "Please sit."

He lifted a dark brow. "I may not be a peer, but I was raised as a gentleman. I can't sit if a lady is standing."

"I'm not a lady."

"All you're missing is the title."

She sat then, because her legs felt unsteady. Caleb had always had a way of making her feel special. She'd thought it was because she was special to him, but she had to resist that sort of thinking now. Now she knew that he was capable of leaving her without even a *fare thee well*. She didn't mean anything more to him than anyone else.

"We have a problem with the search for James," he said without preamble. She'd always liked that about him—he got straight to the point and didn't stall with meaningless pleasantries.

"What is the problem? Did you find something out today?"

"No." He moved closer and put a hand on her shoulder. She realized her voice had risen and her face had grown hot with panic. "I did go to Spitalfields, but I wasn't able to ascertain where exactly the orphanage had been. I admit I was more interested in getting a sense of the place, since I hadn't been in years."

"And?"

"And I realized there's no way for me to do this without calling some attention to myself."

She blinked. "I don't understand."

"There's something I haven't told you."

Bridget shrugged his hand off her shoulder. "That's no surprise. Why start confiding in me now?"

"Don't be a child, Bridget. You know I would have told you if I could have. That was my only request before they sent me. I was denied, and now that I know the full circumstances, I understand the reasoning. I don't like it, but I can't go back and change it now. If I could do it all again, I would defy my orders and tell you everything. You must know that."

She hadn't known that, actually. She hadn't considered that it must have been as hard for him to leave her as it was for her to be separated from him.

"What haven't you told me?"

He sighed and sank onto her bed. Her first reaction was to tell him he couldn't sit there. Not because it was improper; it was beyond improper. But because she didn't want to look at the bed every day and imagine him on it. Imagine herself there with him.

"I'm not living in this boarding house by choice. The Foreign Office put me here."

This made sense. She'd thought they would pay him enough that he could retire to the country if he wished. He could at least afford a decent flat. But if he was still working with the Foreign Office four years after Bonaparte's surrender, something was not right.

"I never told you what I was training for before I left."

"We weren't allowed to talk of such things. I didn't confide details of my work either." No, they'd been too busy with other matters to discuss work overly much. Looking at him sitting on the bed reminded her of those other matters all too easily.

"I think I should tell you something of it now, so you understand my present circumstances and the risk you are taking—the risk I put you in—if we begin this search together."

"I don't care about the risks," she argued. "I'll take any risk necessary if it means I find James."

"Little consolation it will be to find him if you're dead."

Bridget leveled a look at Caleb. "You're right. I think I'd better understand your present circumstances better."

"You must have suspected I was training to be a spy."

She nodded. "Why else the secrecy?"

"You were correct. And when I left you, I infiltrated the ranks of the French. One of the French commanders had an aide-de-camp who died from illness. The commander sent back to France for another man who had been recommended to him. The Foreign Office had that man killed, and I went in his place."

Bridget took a breath. She did not think she would have done anything but worry and fret for Caleb if she'd known these details all those years ago. It had been an incredible risk to take. So much could have gone wrong. "You were accepted?"

"I was able to avoid the few who knew the man I replaced. If I couldn't avoid them, I took other measures."

He'd killed them. The haunted look in his eyes as he remembered was proof enough that he hadn't quite forgiven himself for the sins of war. "I can see you would have been in a unique position to send information back to the Foreign Office."

"Exactly. But I was also in a dangerous position once Napoleon's generals realized they had a spy in their midst. For months, they tried to discover who it was, and I was able to evade them. But no one can escape the noose forever."

Caught up in the story now, Bridget crossed to him and sat on the bed beside him. "How did they catch you?"

"They had suspicions about three or four of us, including me. They held strategy meetings in which only one of the men under suspicion was present at a time. In each meeting, they gave different, false information. When the information I sent was intercepted, they knew who their spy was because they knew who was in the meeting when that false information was given."

"Did they capture you?" Bridget stared into his blue eyes, bright and vivid like the color of a kingfisher's feathers.

"They tried. I escaped and hid all over the Continent for several years. I think, during certain periods, the Foreign Office really did not know whether I was alive or dead. And then the war ended."

She stiffened. This was where he should have come back, found her, saved her from prison, and reunited her with her son.

"I came back. I wanted to look for you, Bridget."

"I wasn't hard to find."

"Neither was I, and that was the problem." He looked down at his hands. "They tried to kill me. They almost succeeded."

"Who?"

"The French army put a price on my head, and even though Napoleon was defeated, my treachery was not forgotten. It still hasn't been forgotten."

If he was still being pursued even four years after the end of the war, he had to be worth a great deal.

"How much?" she asked.

"Ten thousand pounds. Dead or alive."

Her heart sank into her belly. It was a fortune, enough to tempt the most skilled assassins, not to mention the lowest criminals, though she knew Caleb could probably outwit all but the cleverest of men. "Why did you even come back to London? Surely they will expect you to want to return."

"And now you know why I'm biding my time in this fair establishment."

"Except I've asked you to risk your life by searching for my son."

His hand covered hers, large and warm. "Our son. And if there's ever been a worthwhile cause, this is it."

"But?" She should have pulled her hand away, but she didn't. She liked the feel of his strong hand on hers.

"But every criminal in London has probably heard about the price on my head and has seen sketches of me. You won't be safe in my presence."

"Then perhaps it's best if we work quickly."

"I agree." He squeezed her hand. "And once we find the boy, I'll disappear. For good."

*Chapter Four*

Saturday dawned gray and rainy. The rain started as a drizzle, but by the time Caleb led Bridget to Spitalfields, the skies opened in earnest. She'd brought an umbrella, black and battered. It did little to keep her dry, but she came from good Irish stock and wouldn't perish from wet feet in June.

"This is where the orphanage stood," she said, pointing to a corner in Spitalfields. "I think it was a splendid house at one time. It was rather more run-down when I left James here, but it still looked better than most of the places I visited."

Caleb surveyed the debris-strewn lot. "I'm surprised whoever owned it took the time to clear away the burnt husk of the building." He looked about at the dilapidated buildings surrounding them. "There certainly wouldn't have been any penalty for leaving it as it was." He took her arm and steered her away from the lot. "Yesterday, I took some time and looked through various bank records. It appears there was a St. Dismas in Spitalfields, but I can't find records for it after 1816. I assume you already know all of that."

"I do."

She was warm, and her breast pressed against his arm when she moved closer to allow a woman to hurry by. He tried not to notice how she felt beside him. He tried to be a gentleman, but it was damned difficult. "What we want to know is whether the orphanage ceased to exist or reopened with a different name. Something had to be done with those orphans."

She nodded, her movements jerky. Her arm tensed, and he realized he hadn't even considered her greatest fear. "You don't think James is dead, do you?" he asked.

She took a shaky breath. "I don't know. I don't want to believe that. When I asked if anyone died in the fire, I was told there was at least one death."

"It wasn't James." He stopped under a ripped awning and turned her to face him. Her face was so pale, her expression so stricken, he put his gloved hands on either side of her drawn cheeks. "We'll find him. I promise."

"You can't promise that."

"I just did." He wanted to kiss her then. It seemed the most natural thing to do. But she wasn't his any longer. She hadn't been his for a long, long time. "As I see it, we have two options." He let his hands drop because he didn't know if he could resist if he touched her much longer.

"Tell me."

"We risk showing my face to every criminal in the area by visiting every gin house and tavern and asking questions, or we go to the one man who can tell us what we need to know."

"Who is that?"

"Joseph Merceron."

"That's an easy decision. We go to Merceron."

He gave her a tight smile. "You haven't heard of him."

"Should I have?"

"You haven't lived in London's East End, so I wouldn't expect it. He's something of a politician in this area, and nothing happens without him knowing about it. Nothing gets done unless he is paid."

She sighed. "One of those. You can hardly go to him. He's likely to know who you are or be flanked by someone who does."

"I agree. I wouldn't go to him."

She frowned. "But you—" Her eyes widened. "You want me to go to him."

"If we find him in a public place, I think you'd be safe enough. I can stay close by and intervene if there's trouble."

"I'll do it."

Now his brows lifted. "That was a quick agreement."

"If this Merceron knows how to find James, then I'll do whatever it takes."

Caleb swallowed. This was what had made him fall in love with her all those years ago—this strength and single-minded purpose. She was beautiful and intelligent and talented, but more than that, she was strong and loyal. She never thought of herself first. The more time he spent with her now, the more he would fall in love with her all over again.

"There's a tavern he frequents in Bethnal Green. Do you want to go now?"

"By all means. Anything to get out of this rain."

Bridget reconsidered that statement a quarter hour later when she stepped into the Hog and Hen. The place looked as though the hog and hen in question had run rampant through the public rooms. She'd entered by herself about five minutes after Caleb had gone in. He'd told her he'd stand near the bar, and she spotted him easily. She must have looked as uncertain as she felt, because he gave her a firm nod as though to say, *You can do this*.

She took a breath, straightened her shoulders, and moved forward. Of course she could do this. She'd dealt with crying, screaming, fighting ten-year-old girls. A corrupt politician was nothing to her.

She made her way to the bar, aware that several pairs of eyes followed her. She was dressed more…completely than most of the women in the place, but she wasn't here to advertise her charms. Still, her lavender gown and spencer were nothing to make anyone take notice. In an area of Town known for its silk weavers, the cloth of her dress was obviously inferior, as were her battered half boots and her drooping hat. She was nothing to waste time over.

Or so she hoped.

Without looking at Caleb, who was now only a few feet away, she cleared her throat. The barkeep flicked his eyes at her, then went back to polishing a glass. "What can I get you?" he asked flatly.

"Information."

He sighed heavily. "Do I look like a book to you? I don't 'ave no information. I 'ave ale and spirits."

"I need to speak with Joseph Merceron."

The barkeep set the glass on the counter. "What's that to me? Do I look like 'is butler?"

"Where is he?"

The barkeep jerked his head to a dark corner of the tavern, and when Bridget squinted, she spotted an open door that led to another room. "Thank you."

He muttered something under his breath as she walked away. She hoped Caleb followed. She was trembling now, but Satan himself couldn't have stopped her from going into that room. Perhaps she would find James today. She might even hold him in her arms tonight.

She moved through the doorway and into the back room, and a man stepped in front of her. He was short but muscled, his head completely bald. "Can I help you, missus?"

"I'd like to speak with Mr. Merceron."

"Do you owe him blunt?"

"No."

"Then he's busy."

Bridget scowled. "It won't take long. Just a few questions."

"Come back tomorrow. Maybe he'll see you then."

"I can't come back tomorrow. I need to speak with him today. Please."

The man put his hand on her shoulder and, with strength she had no hope of matching, turned her around. "Goodbye, missus."

She walked out and continued walking. Tears burned in her eyes, but she wouldn't give anyone the satisfaction of seeing them.

A few minutes later, Caleb caught up to her. "Bridget! Wait!"

She swiped at her eyes furiously before waiting for him to catch up. She related the conversation.

"So we come back tomorrow." He put a comforting hand on her shoulder.

"And what if he won't see me then?"

"We come back the next day and the next." He pulled her close, and though she knew she should resist, she went willingly, happy to be tucked safely against his side. "Sweetheart, you've been doing this all on your own the past few years. You're not on your own anymore. Together we will find our son."

*Our son.*

Robbie had never referred to James that way. She knew he'd cared for the little boy, but he'd never thought of him as his own son. He'd always spoken of him as *the boy* or *the baby*. Bridget hadn't thought she'd ever want to tell Caleb about his child. She'd done it out of sheer desperation. She was glad she had, because he was right—she had been on her own for a long time. She was grateful to have someone stand beside her and be her partner. Someone who wanted to find James as much as she did.

"You're cold and wet," he said, rubbing a hand up and down her arm. "I'll take you for tea."

"Is it safe for you to be seen in a tea shop?"

"I know one a little out of the way. We'll sit in the back." He took her hand in his and led her down back streets and through alleyways until she was thoroughly lost. Finally, they emerged in front of a small shop she'd never seen before. The sign hanging above the door read Mrs. Scott's Tea Shop. The paint was flaking and the window to the shop rather small, but when Caleb opened the door, a little bell tinkled prettily. Bridget looked around and noted that though the window was small, white lace curtains with cheery yellow sashes framed it. The cozy round tables were covered with lace cloths, and vases of the sort an apothecary might use sat at each table with a single flower inside.

Caleb hung his coat on the stand, then took her wrap and did the same.

A plump woman with doe-brown eyes and a welcoming smile came over and bobbed a curtsy. "Good afternoon, Mr. Smith." She smiled at Bridget. "Table for two today?"

"Thank you, Mrs. Scott. In the back, please."

"Your usual table, then. Right this way." She led them past a scattering of others taking tea. No one paid them any mind. These were not members of the upper echelons of Society—men and women always looking for gossip. These were merchants and tradesmen enjoying a respite on a Saturday afternoon.

They took seats, and Caleb asked for tea and scones. "A bit too early for cakes still," he said when Mrs. Scott departed for the kitchen.

"It's never too early for cake," Bridget retorted.

"You still have a sweet tooth, I see."

"Unfortunately, as I don't have the coin to indulge it very often. The cook at the academy, Mrs. White, makes a delicious trifle on special occasions, though."

He leaned forward, his stunning blue eyes intent on her face. She could have stared into his eyes all day. "I'm not surprised you're teaching now," he said.

"You're not? I've only been at the academy a year."

"I always thought you would make an excellent instructor. You're patient and good at explaining."

Bridget felt her cheeks grow warm. "I like to think I am."

"You were certainly patient with me when the undersecretary asked you to show me how to counterfeit currency."

She had to hide a smile at the memory. How could she have forgotten that?

"Go ahead and laugh. I know I was a poor student."

"You tried very hard, and eventually you caught on."

"I don't have your artistic abilities."

She swallowed at the burst of emotion within, and Mrs. Scott chose that moment to bring a tray with their tea and scones. The tea was hot and strong and the scones absolutely some of the best she'd ever had. They were apple today, and she tasted bits of apple dusted with cinnamon in every bite.

"I have a confession to make," Caleb said after they'd each had a scone and were warm from the tea.

"What's that?"

"I might have pretended to be worse at counterfeiting than I truly was."

"Why would you do that?" But as soon as the words were out of her mouth, she knew the reason.

"I had a fondness for the teacher."

"I confess I didn't mind extra lessons with you."

His gaze on her seemed to warm, and she looked down and took a hasty sip of her tea.

"What about your art?" he asked before the silence could become uncomfortable. "Do you still sketch?"

He really did remember everything about her. For so long, she'd thought she meant nothing to him. More and more, she believed he hadn't wanted to leave without telling her. He'd had no choice.

"Ostensibly, I teach art at the academy. We don't make public the skills like forgery and lockpicking we show the girls. We hope our students will never need them, but we also want them to be prepared for anything. This world is not always easy for females."

"True enough."

"I teach art as well as counterfeiting. When I have James back, I plan to advertise for a few private students to supplement my income."

"That's a clever idea. But when will you have time to create your own art?"

She frowned, perplexed. "I enjoy art, but I don't think my pieces are good enough to sell. I certainly wouldn't make enough to offset the cost of charcoals, pencils, and paper."

He refilled their cups with tea. "I think you're good enough, but regardless, I didn't think you sketched for money. I thought you did it for joy."

Bridget stared at him for a long moment. She hadn't realized how well he understood her.

"Or perhaps I misunderstood," he said when she merely stared at him.

"You didn't misunderstand," she said, feeling self-conscious. When was the last time anyone asked her about herself and what she might like? For years, her life had been about survival.

When had she had time to think about joy? "But drawing for pleasure has not been something I've had the time or funds to do for the past few years."

"Of course not. I wasn't thinking. I apologize."

"Don't. You've made me remember how it once was and how it could be again. I'd lost sight of that."

"You've had other worries. It may not be safe for me to be part of James's life, but you can be assured you both will be taken care of. I have some money saved—"

"Caleb, I don't want your money. That isn't why I asked for help finding him."

"And what if I want to give you money for him? If that's the only way I can be part of his life, at least it's something. I left you to fend for yourself all those years ago. I was well paid for my service, and this is the least I can do."

"I'll think about it."

He didn't press her any further. Instead, he paid for the food and escorted her back to Mrs. Jacobs's. At the corner, where they wouldn't be spotted by the lady herself, he pulled Bridget aside. "I wish I could take you to a museum or Hyde Park."

She looked up at the gray skies and the persistent drizzle. "The park? It's raining."

He gave her a rueful smile. "I wish I could escort you anyway, but I've risked almost enough for one day."

"Almost?"

"Take one more risk with me?"

Years ago, she would have said yes immediately. Now, she hesitated. "What is it?"

"Come to my room after supper tonight. I have something for you."

"What's that?"

"Come to my room and find out." He looked about, then back at her. "Go now. I'll wait a quarter hour and come in after you."

"You should go first."

"I won't have you standing on the street in the rain. Go now, so I can see that you return safely inside."

Bridget nodded and started for the boarding house. She knew there was no point in arguing with Caleb. He was as stubborn as he was honorable. But if he normally took as many chances as he had today, it was a wonder he hadn't been spotted. The city was full of men and women looking for easy money, and Caleb was probably worth more money than she would ever possess.

Bridget greeted Mrs. Jacobs when she entered and went straight to her room. She dropped a few more pieces of the small ration of coal she'd been allotted into the stove and huddled by it for warmth. Later in the summer, it would probably be uncomfortably hot in the room, but today, in her damp clothing, she was cold.

She stripped off her dress and hung it to dry, then did the same with her stays and chemise, wrapping herself in a blanket. She had another chemise that was clean and dry, but it was her best one—a fine lawn with delicate lavender ribbons. She didn't like to wear it often. She took it out of its tissue paper for special occasions.

Did going to Caleb's room qualify as a special occasion? Could she even risk going? It wasn't a ploy to trap her in his chamber and take advantage of her. She knew him too well to ever expect such behavior from him. But that didn't mean she wouldn't be tempted to kiss him if she went. And if she kissed him, she did not know if she'd be able to stop. Or if she'd want him to stop.

Then she might be glad she'd worn her pretty chemise.

The very thought of Caleb seeing her in nothing but the chemise made her throat go dry. She wouldn't decide now. It was still afternoon. She had plenty of time to decide. Instead, she crossed to her bed and pulled out a box from underneath. She opened the box and lifted out several sheets of paper. They were torn and stained from all the times she'd looked at them, all the times they'd been exposed to the elements in Fleet Prison. This was the only possession, other than the clothes on her back, she'd kept in prison.

She lifted the top sheet of paper and stared into the face she'd drawn there. The charcoal sketch depicted a baby smiling sweetly in repose. She remembered watching James sleep and sketching him in the morning light. She'd wondered what he dreamed about when his little brow furrowed or his pink bow of a mouth pursed. He'd been such a beautiful child with his wispy blond hair and large blue eyes, though as an infant, as he was in this sketch, he'd been bald and rosy-cheeked.

The next portrait captured those curls and the eyes. This one was watercolor, and looking at it now, she still didn't think she'd captured the eye color correctly. She'd looked into those same eyes all morning, and paints could hardly do it justice. In the painting, the little boy was reaching for an apple and smiling. His stance was a bit ungainly, as though he might lose his balance and plop onto his bottom at any moment. She traced a hand over the plump cheeks and the dimple in his chin.

The last picture had been difficult to draw and still hurt to look at. She'd drawn it in prison with pencil. It depicted James's head and shoulders as he was carried away from her. One hand reached back as though to grasp her. His face was the picture of misery and terror. Her heart ached when she thought of that day, to know that she'd failed him. Her choices had failed him. She'd thought marrying Robbie would give James a better life. Instead, it had doomed her to prison and sent James to an orphanage.

The room had grown dark, and she put the pictures back into the box and slid them under the bed. She could hear the scrape and click-clacking of silver against china below. Those who had paid for meals were eating downstairs.

Bridget retrieved the bread and cheese Mrs. White had wrapped up for her and ate it slowly, trying to make it last.

When she was done, she lit a candle and read for a while by the flickering light. The house had grown quiet by then. If she was going to go to Caleb's room, now was the time to do it.

She didn't have to go. He would help her regardless. But if she didn't go, she wouldn't know what surprise he had for her. And she'd never know if he still wanted to kiss her, and if she still liked it.

Rising, Bridget took a deep breath and unwrapped her fine chemise.

## Chapter Five

Caleb opened the door at the first knock. He'd been waiting and wasn't too proud to let Bridget know it. He pulled her inside and quickly shut the door, then stepped back so he wasn't tempted to take her into his arms. That wasn't why she'd come.

"I'm glad you're here," he said quietly. The walls were thin, and the house was quiet now.

"I thought about not coming."

"I know. If you hadn't, I would have given you this tomorrow." He lifted a small package from the table and presented it to her.

She took it gingerly and opened the top. "Oh!" The sound came out on a breath. She looked up at him, her brown eyes shining. "I haven't had these since I was a child."

"I thought the same thing when I saw them in the confectioner's. But they're too sweet for me now. They're yours."

"The whole bag?"

"If you can stomach them, yes."

She withdrew a little white piece of sugar fashioned into the shape of a pig and popped it into her mouth. Her eyes closed as she sucked on the sugar. When Caleb's breeches began to feel tight, he had to look away.

"They're just as I remember them," she said. "I could eat the whole bag, but I'll save them for James. It will make a lovely treat when I have him back."

Of course she would save them for James. She never thought of herself. "You eat them, and I'll buy him his own bag."

She set the bag on the table, but didn't release it for a long moment. "I don't mind saving them. Thank you."

"There are at least ten left in the bag. Have one more." He didn't know what made him do it, but he reached for the bag and extracted one of the sugar pigs. Then, though he knew he was playing with fire, he lifted it to her lips.

She didn't part them right away. He touched her lips with the confection, rubbed the sugar against her rosy mouth. Her gaze lifted to his, and he saw the hunger there. Her lips parted, and he slipped the little pig between them. Her pink tongue darted out to take the treat inside. This time, as she sucked it, she didn't close her eyes. Her gaze was hot on his as she stepped closer and slid her arms about his neck. His own arms wrapped around her waist, pulling her against his chest. The feel of her was so natural, so familiar. It was as though no time whatsoever had passed since the last time they had stood like this.

He lowered his head as she angled hers up, and when their lips met, the tremor of desire was palpable.

*This!* his body screamed. *This is what I seek.*

Their mouths fit together as naturally as their bodies, and when his tongue swept inside her mouth, she was as sweet as the confection. He didn't know how long they stood beside the table, feasting. It might have been minutes or hours. But eventually, she broke the kiss and murmured, "Bed."

It took him a moment to comprehend. He stared at her swollen lips, perplexed, then dragged her across the room, lifted her, and placed her on the narrow bed. He had little choice but to come down on top of her. The furnishing was not large enough to accommodate two side by side. Her hands were on his coat, pushing it off his shoulders as he kissed her jaw, her neck, behind her ear.

After several moments of struggling with his coat, she shoved him back. "Take that off."

He sat and she beside him. He stripped off the coat, then loosened his neckcloth. He would have stopped there, but she yanked at his shirt and unfastened the buttons at his neck and sleeves. She stood to pull it off, then looked down at his bare chest. "You have a scar here now." She touched his right shoulder.

"Pistol ball. It went right through."

"And here." She swept her fingers across his left flank.

"Bayonet. I didn't feint fast enough."

Her hand brushed over his abdomen, making him inhale shakily. "You've more muscle than before."

"Staying alive when everyone wants to kill you is hard work. I've been running, fighting, and climbing for years. Give it a few more years and I'll be soft and doughy again."

She smiled, obviously remembering their game. They'd lay in bed for hours, and she'd rest her head on his chest, pretending to mold his belly into dough for bread. Now, he pulled her between his legs. "Kiss me again."

"You don't want to investigate whether I've changed?"

"That depends on whether you want to show me."

She stepped back and reached for the pins holding her bodice together. She wore a dress of cream with pale blue stripes every few inches. The bodice was modest and edged with lace that parted as she removed the pins and dropped them on the floor. The bodice soon followed and then her skirts, until she stood in her chemise and front-lacing stays.

Caleb couldn't sit patiently any longer. He could see the outline of her legs beneath the thin lawn of the shift. The garters of her stockings were purple, like the ribbons of her chemise. He put both hands on her hips and drew her closer. "You're still as beautiful as ever."

"Do you think so?"

Her body had changed. He could feel the swell of hips that had been narrow before, and her breasts all but spilled from the stays when they had been but a small handful when he'd known her years ago.

"I do." He reached up and unlaced the stays, pushing them down over her hips. The hard points of her nipples stood out against the thin fabric of the shift. Caleb's hand skated up her belly to rest between her breasts. Her heart beat fast under his hand. "I've missed you, Bridget. I didn't know how much."

"Show me." She perched herself on his knee and put her arms around him, kissing him slowly and thoroughly. Her lips traced his, then nudged his mouth open. She teased and taunted until he was so hard he had to lean back to alleviate some of the pressure. She tumbled down with him, pushing her hands through his hair and locking her knees about his hips.

He didn't reach for the fall of his breeches. He'd got her with child once, and he wouldn't make that mistake again. Instead, he ran his hands up and down her shift, learning the new curves and revisiting the old. Loosening the ribbon of the chemise, he tugged it down and bared her breasts. As he'd imagined, they were larger, the nipples plumper. He took one in his mouth, and she moaned and pressed her sex against him. It was his turn to moan. As he licked and sucked, she ground against him, causing the sweetest torment.

He took her other breast in his mouth and slid his hands to the hem of her shift. His fingertips grazed her calves and her knees, then up her silky thighs to her plump buttocks. Her eyes opened as he cupped her thighs, and she met his gaze as he slid his hand to the junction of her thighs and the dewy curls nestled there.

He licked her nipple again. "May I touch you here?" His hand brushed over the curls.

"Yes."

Suddenly, he rolled her over. She gave a little shriek before covering her mouth. Then he had her under him. He looked down at her large, dark eyes, her pink cheeks, and her rosy nipples. His hand found the dewy curls again and skated over them. She moaned.

"Shh." He kissed her and moved against her again. She pressed back, welcoming his touch and bringing him into contact with her slick folds. He found her nub of pleasure and, sliding one finger down and over it, entered her. She tightened around him almost immediately, arching to bring him deeper.

He repeated the exercise until they found a rhythm. She was panting, and a sweat had broken out on his brow as he struggled to keep himself in check. He used his tongue to mimic the movements of his hand. Her own tongue tangled with his quickly or slowly, deeply or shallowly, showing him what she wanted.

When her hand clenched on his back, her fingers pressing into the flesh there, he knew she was close. Her hips pumped, and she turned her face into the pillow, and her muscles clenched around his finger. Her climax seemed to last for minutes until she finally took a hitching breath and her hands fell to her sides.

He withdrew his hand and tried not to crush her. He would have liked to lay beside her, but the damn bed was too narrow. He pushed her hair back from her face and kissed her eyes. She opened them and gave him a lazy smile.

"It's been a long time, I think," he said.

"A very long time."

"For me as well."

Her eyebrows rose. "I should do something about that."

He shook his head and held her in place. "Not tonight. Tonight, I just want to hold you."

She gave him a look of surprise, but didn't protest when he shifted to lie on his side. She turned on her side and pressed her face against his chest. He knew most men would have taken her up on her offer. It was tempting. He'd taught her how to use her mouth, and he knew she could please him—more than please him. But he'd been alone for so long. He'd been running for so long, and he hadn't realized how much he missed holding a woman. How much he missed the companionship of a long conversation. How tired he was of his cold, lonely bed.

She was warm and smelled faintly of orange blossoms. Her skin was soft where he rubbed a hand over it. Soon, her breathing grew deeper and more even. She slept in his arms, and he was more content than he'd been in years.

Bridget awoke in her own bed. She remembered Caleb waking her, helping her dress, and escorting her back to her own room. It wouldn't do for her to be seen coming out of his chambers in the morning. But she hadn't slept well after she'd come back to her room. She'd slept much better pressed against him in the tiny bed. She liked the way the hair on his chest tickled her cheeks and the way his hands kept her nestled close and safe.

Today was Sunday, and she usually attended church services in the chapel at the academy. A few eyebrows might lift if she did not attend, so she dressed for church in a gown of white with peach ribbons at the bodice and sleeves and made her way to Manchester Square. She found Valérie and sat beside her just as the girls began to sing the first hymn.

"Did you find him yet?" Valérie asked.

For a moment, Bridget thought her friend meant Caleb, and then she realized Valérie meant James. "Not yet," she whispered, "but I am close." That was true enough. She would go to see Merceron again after church today. Perhaps he would not be as busy on the Sabbath.

Valérie squeezed her hand, clearly excited for her. After the service, Bridget hugged Valérie and started for the front door. Irene Chalmers called out to her before she could reach the door. With her curly black hair, light brown skin, and dark eyes, she was truly lovely. She was also amazingly intelligent, teaching history, geography, and pocketpicking.

"Mrs. Chalmers, it was a lovely service, wasn't it?"

"It was. You're not leaving without dinner, are you?" She leaned close and lowered her voice. "I know Mrs. White is still finding her footing, but she's made some delicious meals recently."

"I'd like to, but I have business to attend to."

"I see. Then I'd better mention this now. I have a cousin with a daughter of about nine. She thinks the little girl shows some aptitude for drawing. I told her you would be giving lessons on Saturdays soon. Do you still plan to do so?"

Bridget smiled. "Yes! And thank you for thinking of me. I think in another week or two, I will be ready to begin lessons."

"I'll tell her. She may have friends, and if her mother likes you, I'm sure she'll refer them to you."

"Irene, you're an angel. Thank you."

"You're welcome. At least grab a slice of toast from the kitchen before you go. You have to eat something."

Bridget took her advice, smiling all the way back to Covent Garden. If she could find just four or five regular art students, she would be able to supplement her income from the academy nicely and afford clothing and shoes for James and perhaps pay her debt to her great-aunt more quickly. She hadn't yet decided if she would accept money from Caleb, but if she did, that could be used to pay for tutors and schooling, though she was in no hurry to send her son off to school. He could attend a school here in London and live at home, as many of the sons of merchants and tradesmen did.

Caleb had told her to wait for him near the theater, and she spotted him almost immediately. It might be more apt to say she spotted him as soon as he allowed it. She'd been looking for him outside the theater as she approached and thought she had arrived early. Then he seemed to appear from nowhere. He joined her, falling into step beside her.

Seeing him again brought the memories of the night before rushing back. The way his kingfisher-blue eyes had looked up at her as she'd disrobed, the way his mouth had looked when he kissed her breast, the way his hands had felt as they touched her. She felt her cheeks heat at the memory.

"Are you feeling suddenly shy?" he asked after the silence had gone on and he'd glanced at her face.

"Just remembering last night."

"I'm sure you repented this morning."

He turned in the direction of Bethnal Green. "Did you?" she asked.

"Hell no. I'm not a bit sorry."

She laughed. "You are incorrigible."

"I am. I see you in that pretty dress and jaunty hat, and all I can think about is taking it off you."

Now her cheeks heated for another reason. She swallowed, eager to change the subject. "I have good news."

"Tidings of great joy? Isn't that in December?"

She punched him lightly. "Not that good news. A young girl is interested in taking art lessons with me. If her mother recommends me to her friends, I could soon have a number of pupils."

"And what will you do with all that blunt?"

"Buy James clothes and shoes and pay for schooling."

"Are you still determined not to accept my money?"

She ducked her head. "I suppose if you are determined to give it to me, I won't refuse. I could move to better accommodations or buy James some toys."

He took her hand and squeezed it. "We'll find him today. I can feel it."

She nodded, not wanting to allow her expectations to rise too high. At the Hog and Hen, she knew where to go and what to do. She entered right before Caleb and made her way to the back room. She waited until Caleb took a seat at a table nearby, then approached the entrance to the room, where the same sentry as the day before stood.

"Can I help you, missus?"

"Yes, you can. I'd like to speak with Mr. Merceron."

He scratched his bald head. "Do you owe him blunt?"

"No."

"Then—"

"But I'll pay him for information."

The sentry's brows went up. "What sort of information?"

"I'll discuss that with Mr. Merceron." She tried to move past the sentry, but he blocked her path.

"Come back tomorrow. Maybe he'll see you then."

"That's what you told me yesterday." She rose on tiptoe and spotted a well-dressed man sitting at a table with another man and speaking in hushed tones. "Mr. Merceron!" she called, hoping he was the man at the table.

He looked up, glancing from her to his man, then back to her.

"I need to speak to you, sir."

"Oy!" The sentry moved to block her vision. "I say who sees Mr. Merceron." He grabbed her arm and pushed her around, and immediately Caleb was at his side.

"You'll want to release the lady," he said, voice low and menacing.

"And who are you?"

"A friend of the lady."

By this time, Merceron had risen. As she'd observed, he was well-dressed, though his clothes were too bright and too flashy to be those of a nobleman. His dark hair was pulled back into a queue, and he had a high forehead and a large, flat nose. It had obviously been broken a time or two. "What's this about, Digsby?"

"I told this wench to be on her way, but her cull is giving me trouble."

Merceron's gaze flicked to Caleb, then back to Bridget. He gave her a quick once-over. "I must apologize for Digsby, missus. Is there something I can help you with?"

Digsby scowled, but stepped back and out of the way.

"I'm looking for Joseph Merceron."

"You've found him." He gave a half bow. "Come sit."

Caleb made to retreat, but Merceron pointed at him. "You too, fellow. Come and have a drink."

Bridget shot Caleb an apologetic look, then took the seat Merceron offered. His previous companion was gone. Since he hadn't passed Bridget on his way out, she surmised there must be a back door. Caleb took a seat as well, keeping his hat pulled low over his brow.

"Do I know you?" Merceron asked Caleb. "You look familiar."

"I've lived here and there," Caleb answered.

Merceron lifted the bottle of wine on the table. "Thirsty?" he asked Bridget.

"No, thank you. I actually have a question to ask you. I'm told you're familiar with Spitalfields."

He nodded. "I was born on Brick Lane. I know every inch of that street, from Spitalfields to Bethnal Green. You want to open a business?"

"No. Actually, I'm looking for someone. He was left at the St. Dismas Home for Wayward Youth, but that building has burned down."

"Happened about three years ago. One of my men was injured in the fire. He was trying to help the women and children escape, of course."

"Of course," Caleb muttered.

"But it weren't called St. Dismas. That rum mort who took over named it something else."

"What's that?"

Merceron crossed his arms and smiled. "I don't rightly remember."

Caleb put a penny on the table. Merceron looked at the penny, then tapped his forehead.

Caleb put two more pennies on the table.

"Now it's coming to me. Sunnyvale or Sunnybrooke Home for Boys."

"Where is it located now?" Caleb asked.

"Not in my jurisdiction, so I don't care. But the rum mort…what was her name?"

Caleb sighed and put another penny on the table.

"Lady Julia. That's right. She was the daughter of a duke or an earl or one of them nobs. I assumed she either went back to her ballroom or moved the orphanage somewhere a bit to the west."

Caleb stood, and Bridget followed. "Thank you."

Merceron looked up at Caleb. "Sure I don't know you?"

"I'm sure." He hurried Bridget through the tavern, and when they stepped outside, he muttered, "I shouldn't have come with you. He knows who I am."

## Chapter Six

Caleb knew the moment Merceron said he looked familiar that he'd made a mistake. He didn't regret going with Bridget. He couldn't have sent her into the tavern alone, and he'd known it was a risk to go along. But now he could feel the shadow of danger closing in.

Bridget, on the other hand, was blissfully unaware of the peril awaiting them. She was walking quickly and chattering about the new information they'd gained. He did not wish to ruin her excitement, but he thought the sooner he separated from her, the better.

"Should we find a bookstore and purchase a directory? Surely there can't be too many orphanages with *sunny* in the name."

"I don't know that a directory of businesses or tourist sites would list orphanages at all."

Her shoulders fell. "You're correct, of course." She looked up at the sky, which was cloudy, but at least no rain fell. "I suppose we can start in Mayfair and ask people we meet if they know it."

He steered her toward a shop window, the blinds pulled down indicating it was closed on Sunday. "We might find it even more quickly if we go to the charity hospital. The nurses will know all the foundling houses."

She nodded. "Yes. I didn't think of that. Let's go now." She started away, but he grasped her arm lightly, holding her back. "What's wrong?"

"I can't go with you. In fact, it's time we say goodbye."

The excitement and pleasure on her face fled. "I don't understand. We're so close."

"You are. I have no doubt you'll find James today, but not if I'm with you. I'll only cause you trouble."

She shook her head. "No, you won't. I understand if you don't want James to know who you are, but there's no reason you can't meet him."

He bent close to her. "I was recognized, Bridget. Merceron knew my face. He might not have put my face with my name and the reward offered for me, but he will. And when that happens, he'll send men after me. I have to leave Mrs. Jacobs's, choose a new name, and find another place to hide. London is full of boarding houses and taverns with rooms to let. It won't be difficult."

"And that's to be your life? Always running? Always hiding?"

He straightened. "If I want to live, yes. I had thought—" He shook his head. "You should go on without me."

"Finish what you were saying."

"It's nothing that concerns you. I'd thought of leaving, sailing for the Americas or Canada. I'd be safe there."

She stepped back, knocking into the window. "That's so far away."

"I should have gone already, but there was something keeping me here." He looked into his eyes. "Someone. Now that I know you are safe and well and will be provided for, I can go. I'll leave blunt under your pillow before I go, enough to see that you and James are cared for." He took her hand and kissed it. "I've never loved anyone else, Bridget. I don't think I ever will."

It was the hardest thing he'd ever done, to walk away. He heard her harsh intake of breath and the sob as she released it, but he didn't look back. If he truly cared for her, walking away from her was the right thing to do. And he'd be damned if he would put her and his child in danger.

He turned a corner and stumbled. Every fiber of his being wanted to go back to her, but he forced himself forward, returning to Mrs. Jacobs's. He'd gather his things, leave Bridget the blunt, and be on his way. Perhaps it was best if he left England altogether. If he was in the same city, he didn't trust himself not to attempt to sneak a look at Bridget or James. It would be better if an ocean separated them, safer for all of them.

Two hours later, Bridget trudged up the stairs of Mrs. Jacobs's boarding house. She was tired and hot and discouraged. By the time she reached the second floor, she was also lightheaded. She hadn't eaten since the pilfered slice of bread after church, and that had been hours ago.

She unlocked her door, stepped into her dark room, and leaned back against the door. The rain from the day before had left the city muggy and humid, and this upper chamber was as stuffy as she'd known it would be. She started for the window, then paused and glanced at her bed. Had Caleb left the money under her pillow? She turned back, then screamed when she saw the man standing on the other side of the room.

Caleb stood, hands outstretched. "It's only me, Bridget."

She clamped a hand over her mouth and stared at him. "I thought you were gone," she whispered.

"I tried to leave, but they'd already found me."

"Who? How?"

A sharp tap at the door startled her into silence. "Mrs. Lavery? Are you well?" Mrs. Jacobs asked.

She winced, then motioned for Caleb to get behind the door. "I'm fine, Mrs. Jacobs," Bridget called. But she knew that wouldn't satisfy the lady, so she went to the door and opened it a crack. "I'm so sorry. I thought I saw a rat."

Mrs. Jacobs stabbed her hands on her hips. "All that racket because you saw a rat! I thought you'd been set on by murderers.

First, those men looking for Mr. Smith, now this." She started away, but Bridget slid out the door and went after her.

"What men looking for Mr. Smith?"

"Not that it's any of your business, but three men came here looking for him. They said they were from the magistrate and he'd stolen something. Asked to search his room, but when they went in, lo and behold, he had already cleared out. Thieves and whores have taken over the city, I tell you."

"Where are these men now?"

"How should I know?" Her eyes narrowed. "What's it to you?"

"I just wondered how you could be certain they came from the magistrate. Was the magistrate with them?"

"How I could be certain? How I could be—do you think men just go about impersonating city officials? Why, that's the most ridiculous thing I've ever heard."

Bridget nodded. "I suppose you're right."

"Course I'm right." She pointed a finger at Bridget. "No more screams out of you."

"No, madam. Again, I'm sorry." She went back to her room, closing the door quietly and locking it. Caleb stood against the wall, arms crossed.

"I was in here when they arrived." He gestured to a valise near her table. "I thought I'd better wait to leave until it was safe."

"When will that be?"

"After dark. I doubt they left anyone to watch the place, since it was clear I'd already taken my belongings and gone, but I don't want to risk being seen."

"Should I go out and look around?"

He crossed to her and put his hands on her arms. "No. Stay inside. I've been sitting here the past hour worrying about you. Where is James?"

She closed her eyes, and he led her to the bed, sitting beside her. "I didn't find him. I went to the hospital, but no one was there to see me today. It's Sunday, and only a few nurses were working, and they had more work than they could handle. I was told to come back tomorrow."

"Then you go back tomorrow."

"I have to teach tomorrow and won't be able to go back until evening."

He stroked her hair. "I know it's difficult to wait."

She nodded. "I just want to see him, hold him, know he's all right. I know one more day is nothing after all these years, but it feels like forever." She swiped at her eyes. "And now I'm crying. I don't know what's wrong with me."

"You're tired, and you haven't eaten. I have bread and apples in my valise."

He rose and fetched them, tossing them in the center of her small bed. "You need these for your travels," she said.

"I'll buy more. Eat."

She lifted an apple and bit in while he dug under her pillow and produced a handful of paper notes. "For you and James." He pressed them into her hand.

Bridget gaped at them. "Five pounds? I can't accept this. It's too much."

"Then accept it for James."

She nodded and secreted the notes in a drawer. "I have something for you as well," she said, returning to the bed. She reached underneath and pulled out the box. "I would have shown you these before, but I didn't realize you'd have to leave so soon."

She opened the cover and drew out the sketch of James when he'd been an infant. "I drew these of our son." She handed him the first one and watched his face as he studied it. His expression turned from wonder to joy to pride.

"He's beautiful. Like his mother."

"More like his father." She handed him the second drawing. "He has your eyes."

Caleb touched a finger to the drawing. "He does." He looked up at her. "He really does."

"I don't think I got the color quite right." She placed a hand on his temple. "But then, I don't think anyone could. Did you mean it?" she asked.

His brow furrowed.

"When you said you'd never loved anyone else. Did you mean that you loved me?"

"I still love you."

She swallowed her uncertainty. "Then don't go. I want us to be a family."

"Bridget, you know that's not possible. The only way to keep you safe is to leave you. I've already put you in danger."

"There's no reason for anyone to come after me."

"And I don't want to give them one." He looked down at the box. "Do you have any more drawings?"

"Just one." She lifted the last, the drawing that showed James crying as he was taken away from her. Caleb took it and let out a slow breath.

"Bridget, I'm so sorry."

"It wasn't your fault."

"It was. I swear to you, this will never happen again. I'll make sure you always have funds."

"I'll be fine. I have my position at the academy and students waiting for art lessons. James and I will be fine. I don't need your money." She took the drawing from his hand and placed it with the others back in the box. "I just need you."

Still on her knees, she put her arms around his neck and kissed him. If she was not to see him again, then she wanted one last night to remember him by. He kissed her back, tentatively at first and then with more passion. She pulled his coat off and unfastened his neckcloth, making it clear she wanted more than his hand on her tonight. She wanted all of him.

"Are you certain?" he asked when she reached for the placket of his breeches.

"Absolutely certain." She loosed the breeches and took him in her hand. He was warm and hard, the weight of him familiar. She stroked him, then pushed him back on the bed and lifted her skirts to climb on top of him. He grasped her waist, staying her.

"If we're to do this, I want to do it right."

She raised her brows. "I thought I *was* doing it right."

"I want you naked. I want to see you."

"Then undress me."

He lifted her off him and stripped his own clothes off first. Bridget's throat went dry at the sight of him—his long, muscled legs; his broad shoulders; his corded arms.

He started with her hair, plucking pins from the simple upsweep until it all tumbled about her shoulders. Then he unfastened the bodice of the dress, slid the skirts and petticoats off, and gave her a long look as she stood in only her chemise and stays.

"Are you tired already?" she asked.

"Just trying to decide what to take off next. I could remove your garters and stockings, but perhaps I should leave those for last and divest you of your stays and shift first."

She stepped out of her shoes, pushed them aside, and put her arms around his waist. His hard member pushed against her belly, and he inhaled sharply when her hands squeezed his buttocks. "Or you could just take me now and worry about the clothing later."

"Tempting as that sounds, I want to see all of you. Stays first, I think." He pushed her gently back and unlaced her stays, then tugged at the hem of her chemise. Pulling it over her head, he dropped it on the floor. She felt suddenly self-conscious, standing there in nothing but her stockings and garters, but as soon as she looked at him, all traces of embarrassment fled. There was nothing but desire and heat in the way he looked at her. His gaze was almost reverent.

"Let's get those stockings off," he said, voice husky. He took her hand and led her to the bed. She sat, and he spread her legs, kneeling between them. He took one foot, lifted it, and slid his other hand up her calf to just above her knee where her black garters secured her white stocking. He lowered the garters, then rolled the stocking down very slowly. Bridget trembled, then struggled to catch her breath as he set her bare foot on his shoulder and turned to her other leg. He didn't lift that one, though. Instead, he bent and kissed the bare flesh above her knee. His lips slid upward, and she was all but panting.

His mouth moved farther up her thigh, and she leaned back, catching herself on her elbows. He spread her legs farther and pressed his mouth where her legs joined her torso. Her hands clenched on the rough blanket as his lips slid over and his tongue lapped at the delicate flesh. When he found the bud that gave her pleasure, she shook so badly, she lay flat, giving herself up to his ministrations.

She'd forgotten this. She'd forgotten how well he pleasured her with his mouth. He could draw it out for hours, making her climax over and over, until she thought she had nothing left. His tongue was gentle, teasing and testing. He spread her legs wider and circled her, pulling back when she came too close to peaking.

"Please," she begged in a whisper, because she feared if she spoke any louder, she might scream. "I want you inside me."

"Patience," he murmured, beginning his teasing again. Her breathing grew rapid until she was gasping and clawing at the blanket. Finally, finally, he pressed his tongue deliberately against her sensitive bud, and she came apart. Just as she began to descend, he drove into her, and she soared higher again. She bit her lip to keep from crying out. Caleb wasn't gentle, and she didn't want him to be. She wrapped her legs around him, pulling him deeper. Finally, he tensed and cried out, withdrawing quickly and spilling himself on her belly.

He fell beside her, chest rising and falling. When he'd recovered, he found a cloth, cleaned her, then lay beside her again and pulled her close. "I've missed you." He buried his face in her hair and stroked her shoulder.

"I've missed you." She turned to look at him. For all these years, she'd held her memories of him locked away in the back of her mind. She hadn't wanted to take them out and examine them, because he'd left her. But now she knew he hadn't left her out of choice but duty. And the time she'd spent with him these past days, along with the past they'd shared, swirled together. "I don't want you to go." She placed a hand on his cheek. "I love you."

He stilled. "I didn't think you'd say it again. I didn't know if you'd trust me."

"I trust you. I know you only want to protect me and James. If we can't be together in London, what if we traveled with you to somewhere safe?"

Caleb shook his head. "Long sea voyages can be dangerous. There are storms and mercenaries."

She kissed him. "The streets of London can be dangerous as well. Together we will keep each other safe."

He lay back and stared at the ceiling for so long she thought he would deny her. Then finally, he rose on one elbow. "I should tell you no."

"But you won't."

"I won't. But we must find James tomorrow. We need to leave on the first ship where I can book passage."

## Chapter Seven

He'd left her well after midnight. It had been no easy feat to force himself away from the warmth of her body and the sweet perfume of her skin. But if anyone was watching the boarding house, he had to leave under cover of darkness or risk being caught.

Caleb had gone out the back door, through the kitchen, and into a back alley. From there, he'd made his way to the docks, avoiding the main thoroughfares and keeping to the side streets as much as possible.

He'd found a ship bound for Canada via Ireland. The captain had no cabins left, but he offered Caleb first choice of vacated cabins once they reached the isle. Caleb paid the fare for three and hoped Bridget thought sleeping under the stars for a night or two romantic.

It was easy to hide in the taverns and warehouses that lined the docks. No one looked too closely at a man here, and most men kept their hats down low and their eyes on their own business.

At two o'clock, he started back into the city toward the charity hospital. Bridget had said she'd ask another teacher to take her afternoon classes so she could go to the hospital. He'd meet her outside, and they'd go to the orphanage together.

He walked quickly, keeping an eye over his shoulder. When he arrived at the hospital, he waited across the street from it, tucking himself behind the pillar of a building. He'd been waiting about a quarter of an hour when Bridget entered. She wore her cream and peach dress and a hat to match. Her hair was in curls over one shoulder, and she looked as pretty as he'd ever seen her.

He ducked back behind the pillar, allowing himself a few moments to imagine their life together. He'd marry her as soon as possible. Perhaps they could get a license when the ship docked in Ireland. He wanted to be her husband. He was already a father. He still couldn't believe he was the father of the beautiful child she'd shown him in the drawings last night. Had she just imagined the resemblance the boy bore to Caleb, or did he really look like his father?

He'd find a position in the government of Canada. He knew how government offices worked. Bridget could give drawing lessons, and they'd find a school for James. There would be more children—girls and boys who would bring them joy and perhaps frustrate them as well. He wouldn't have to watch his back any longer. He wouldn't have to hide.

Caleb glanced out from behind the pillar, watching the door to the hospital more keenly now. A few minutes later, Bridget emerged. She looked about, and he stepped out from the pillar long enough for her to spot him before ducking back again. Her face had broken into a beatific smile, and he knew without having to be told that she had the information she wanted.

"I know where he is," she said, darting behind the pillar. "Rather, where the orphanage is. I suppose there's no guarantee James will still be there." She told him the street, and he nodded. It was in a prosperous area of Town, but that didn't mean he could relax his guard.

"Did you book passage?" she asked.

"Yes. We go to Ireland, then Canada."

She nodded, looking both excited and scared. "I took my things to the academy this morning. I can send word to have them sent to the dock. I didn't want to trust Mrs. Jacobs to do it. She'd probably charge me for her troubles."

"There's no doubt of that. Shall we go collect James?"

She took a deep breath. "Yes."

Caleb led the way, keeping her arm tucked in his and his head down. He still avoided the main streets, but the back alleys were mostly mews once they reached the West End.

"Two more blocks and we should reach it," she said.

"You'll finally see him again."

She gripped his arm tightly, and he paused, glancing about at the grooms moving horses in and out of stables around them. No one seemed to be paying them much mind.

"What if he doesn't remember me? He was so young."

Caleb thought it unlikely the boy would remember her. "Then you start off as friends and earn his trust, and his love will follow."

"He won't be the same little boy I knew. He'll be eight years old. I've missed so much."

He squeezed her arm. "You did what you had to. You won't miss a day more."

She took a deep breath, then made a face because the air smelled strongly of manure. "I'm ready."

They started forward, but had gone no more than two or three steps when two men stepped out from behind one of the buildings. Caleb stopped, pulling Bridget close to him. She immediately saw the danger and turned to go back the way they'd come, but two more men stepped into their path. "I'll distract them," he murmured. "You run to the orphanage. I'll meet you. If I don't, go back to the academy. You'll be safe there."

"But—"

He didn't wait for her to finish. He pushed her aside and ran for the two men in front of them. Taken by surprise, they fell back, and Caleb got in several punches before they came at him. Bridget tried to go around, but just as she had a clear path, the men approaching from the rear went for her.

Caleb let out a yell, broke away from the men he'd been fighting, and tackled one of the men after Bridget. He was surrounded now, four against one. The odds were not in his favor, but amid the volley of fists, he saw Bridget running toward the orphanage.

She didn't stop until she reached the Sunnybrooke Home for Boys. Even then, she couldn't stop expecting the men who'd attacked Caleb to catch up to her. When they didn't leap out from around the corner, she pressed herself against the wall and took several deep breaths. It wouldn't do to arrive winded and disheveled.

She smoothed her skirts and hair, slowed her breathing, and said a quick prayer for Caleb. If those men killed him, it would be her fault. She'd persuaded him to take her with him. He could have been safely on a ship already if not for her.

Swallowing her fear, she tapped on the door and waited. Nothing happened, so she knocked more firmly. A moment later, she heard footsteps, and a young woman in a dress and apron opened the door. "Can I help you?"

"I'm here about a boy. I had to leave him with this orphanage about five years ago. Now I've come to take him back."

The maid blinked in surprise. Clearly, this did not happen often. Finally, she opened the door wider and motioned for Bridget to enter. "You'll be wanting Lady Julia, I think. Come sit in the parlor while I fetch her."

Bridget stepped inside a well-lit circular foyer surrounded by doors. One was open, and she could see the dining room, where the maid who'd opened the door must have been cleaning when Bridget had knocked. The room boasted two long tables where the children took meals. Windows looked out onto the street, and landscapes adorned the white, clean walls. Steps led to the upper floors. They were carpeted and bracketed by wooden railings that gleamed in the afternoon sunshine. If she hadn't known this was a home for orphans, she would have thought it an academy like the one where she taught.

"Where are the children?" Bridget asked.

"The older ones are at their lessons, and the littles are up from their naps and having their tea." She opened another door that led into a room painted pale blue. Comfortable chairs upholstered in cream damask were set in an inviting arrangement. "Wait here. May I ask the name of the child you seek?"

Bridget cleared her throat. "James. James Lavery."

The maid furrowed her brow as though she didn't know the name, but bobbed and closed the door. Bridget stood with her hands clasped as the sound of the woman's shoes grew fainter and fainter. What if he wasn't here? What if she and Caleb had risked everything and James wasn't here? And Caleb—she'd left him fighting four men. What if he did not come to the orphanage? What if she lost both James and Caleb today?

Bridget crossed the small room to a window covered with white lace and framed by light blue draperies. She moved the lace aside and looked out on a small garden with ample room for boys to play. Indeed, several balls and a croquet set were spread about the lawn. Bridget prayed James would be here. Not only because she wanted to find him, but because she could see this was the sort of place where children were loved and cared for.

The door opened, and she spun around. A woman of medium height with coppery-red hair and large brown eyes stepped inside. "Good afternoon." She had an upper-class accent, and the navy and white gown she wore was of the best quality. "I am Lady Julia. I've run Sunnybrooke these past four years."

Bridget crossed to her and shook her hand. "Bridget Lavery. I left my son at St. Dismas about five years ago. My husband and I were to be sent to Fleet Prison, and I didn't want James to suffer with us."

"I see." She gestured to the chairs, and Bridget sat on the edge of one. "Shall I ring for tea?"

"That's not necessary, my lady. I just came for James. I paid off my debt, and I have a good job now and a place of my own. I've been looking for him, but the old orphanage wasn't there."

"It burned down, yes." She lifted a file she held. "Sanders said you wanted James, but I think the boy you mean is the one we call Jimmy."

"Jimmy, yes. We called him that when he was little." Bridget's chest tightened. "He's still here?"

"He is." She opened the file folder. "James Lavery was surrendered by his mother, Bridget, and his father, Robert, in 1814. Are you Bridget?"

"Yes."

"And Robert?"

"He passed away in prison. To tell you the truth, he wasn't James—Jimmy's real father. His real father couldn't be here this afternoon. He had some…government business to attend to. But he wants us to be a family, as do I."

"Jimmy's father works for the government?"

"You could say that. In fact, we're thinking of sailing to Canada. I know it would be a big change for Jimmy." She was rambling now, but she was so nervous and anxious to see Jimmy.

"It would, but he's an adventurous boy. I don't think he'd have trouble adapting." She closed the folder. "He's always said you would come back for him. I don't think any of us believed him, but here you are."

"Then you'll let me have him?"

"If he wants to go with you, yes. Everything you've said matches what I have in the file, even your description. I rarely see happy endings like this." She rang a bell. "Let's fetch him, shall we?"

The door opened, and the maid, Sanders, entered. "Yes, my lady?"

"Will you ask Jimmy to come down, please?"

"Jimmy?" Her eyes darted to Bridget. "Certainly, my lady." She closed the door, and Bridget let out a shaky breath.

"You're nervous. Don't be. He's a wonderful boy. He's been waiting for you."

"He's been waiting a long time. I was afraid he'd think I forgot about him."

"There might have been days when he felt that way, but a mother's love can heal those small wounds."

The sounds of thumping feet on the stairs drew their attention. "Ah, here he comes."

Bridget stood, visibly trembling now. She'd never been so frightened in all her life. She clenched her hands together until her nails bit into her palms.

A knock sounded on the door, and then Sanders opened it, and a boy just over four feet with straight brown hair and bright blue eyes stepped inside. His gaze passed over Bridget and went straight to Lady Julia. "What's wrong, my lady?"

Lady Julia smiled at him. "Nothing, Jimmy. In fact, I have very good news."

His brows rose expectantly.

"For years, you've been saying your parents were in debtor's prison and would come back for you." He nodded. "This is your mother." She gestured to Bridget. "She's come back."

The boy's eyes flicked to Bridget, and she clasped her hands together so tightly it hurt. She tried to manage a smile, but it wobbled, and she felt tears in her eyes. "James—Jimmy," she said.

"I'm your mother, Bridget Lavery. I've been looking for you for a long time."

He stared at her, and she could see that he was working to try to remember her. She was trying to take the face she saw before her now and fit it against what she remembered of him as a baby. His face had grown and matured, but the eyes were the same, as was the nose and the expression he gave her. His hair had darkened, as she'd expected, and he looked fit and healthy.

"You're my mother?"

She nodded. "I've been looking for you."

He took a step closer. "Where's my father?"

She looked down. "I'm afraid the man I was married to when you were born passed away in Fleet Prison. But your real father would very much like to meet you. He's back from the war now, and you have his eyes."

He touched his brow and took another step closer. "I do?"

"The very same." A sob escaped her best efforts to hold it back. "James, I'm so sorry I had to leave you here. I'm so, so sorry. I don't know how you can forgive me, but if you'll let me, I'll never leave you again. I'll be a good mother to you."

He ran into her arms and hugged her fiercely. "Don't cry. I know you didn't want to do it. I knew you'd be back."

Bridget cried all the harder because *he* was comforting *her*. "I never stopped loving you." She took his face in her hands. "Never. Not for a day or an hour or a minute. I thought of you always."

"I thought of you too, Mama." He hugged her again, and she pulled him tight against her. They stayed like that for a long time. Bridget didn't ever want to let him go. She had him in her arms again, those arms that had ached in their emptiness were filled once more.

"You smell the same," he said quietly. She drew back and looked at him. "I don't remember what you looked like, but I remember how you smelled. It's the same." Tears shimmered in his blue eyes, and she kissed them away.

"Jimmy," Lady Julia said quietly. "Your mother would like you to go with her. In fact, I think she and your father have plans to travel to Canada. Do you want to go with her? You don't have to go tonight. You can think about it. Take a few days to decide."

Bridget took a deep breath. Caleb didn't have a few days, but she could hardly force the child to leave everything he'd known at a moment's notice.

"I want to go," he said. "But can I say goodbye to everyone first?" He looked at Bridget.

"Of course. Tell them you'll write and send presents from your travels."

He smiled. "I will! I'll be right back. Don't leave without me."

She sat in one of the chairs. "I won't move from this seat."

He ran up the stairs, his shoes clomping loudly, and Lady Julia shook her head. "I'll go pack his things." She wiped one eye.

"I'll miss him, and if anything ever happens, know that you can bring him back with no questions asked."

"Thank you. And thank you for taking such good care of him."

Lady Julia nodded and left Bridget alone. Bridget pulled a handkerchief from her sleeve and wept.

## Chapter Eight

He'd fought as hard as he could until Bridget was safely away, and then he'd fought more. In the end, he was no match for four men. They'd bound him and dragged him away, all while startled grooms watched.

"I haven't done anything to you," Caleb argued as they shoved him inside a coach. "Let me go."

"You've got a price on your head," one of the men said. "And we all get a portion once you're delivered."

"I'll pay you," he offered as they wrestled him inside the conveyance.

"How much?"

"A guinea each."

"We'll make ten each when you're delivered."

They drove him to a house. He didn't see where, as the coach's curtains were drawn, but he knew they hadn't traveled long enough to be out of London. They hauled him out, marched him through the empty house, shut him in an empty room, and locked the door.

Caleb sat on his heels and reached his bound hands into his boot, drawing out the knife there. The hired men hadn't searched him, and that was their mistake. He had a few hours to make the most of their oversight, because the men who were coming for him wouldn't make mistakes. He'd be dead by morning.

As Caleb struggled to turn the knife to a useful position, he studied the light coming through the drawn curtains. It was late afternoon now. Had Bridget found the orphanage? Had she found their son?

He finally had the blade in position and began to work it against his bindings. The rope was thick, and it would take time to cut through it. It was time he didn't have. He desperately wanted to meet his son, to see Bridget again, to board that ship to Canada. The government might come looking for him, especially if what the grooms saw in the West End was made public. But by the time they tracked him down, he'd have washed up on the side of the Thames.

He had to cut these ropes. He sawed with renewed vigor, his fingers growing sweaty, until he dropped the knife.

James—Jimmy had held her hand all the way back to the academy. It had seemed the most natural thing in the world to walk with his hand in hers, keeping him close to her side and safe from the coaches on the streets.

She carried his valise, which she didn't think was his at all. It looked very much like the sort a lady of the *ton* might own. And that was just another kindness Lady Julia had done them.

"Will my father be waiting for us at this school?" Jimmy asked.

"I hope so, but I don't know. He was a hero during the war, and now London is dangerous for him. That's why we hope to go to Canada."

"My father is a hero?"

"Yes. He was very important during the war. He might not be able to meet us if it's too dangerous. In that case, we'll stay in London. I have a room and enough money to buy us food and clothing and pay for your schooling."

"I have clothing," he said. "Lady Julia always made sure we had clothing. This shirt used to be Michael's. I don't know who the trousers belonged to. The shoes are new, though. Lady Julia says we boys are hell on shoes." He squeezed her hand. "But don't tell her I said the H-word. I'm not allowed to say it."

Bridget squeezed his hand back. "I won't tell." As she looked down at him, a wave of love swept over her. He was so sweet, so good, so beautiful. She'd never thought she'd have him back, but now that she did, she would never, never let him go.

Finally, just before dusk, they reached the academy. She led Jimmy inside and took him straight to the kitchens. Mrs. White was counting the silver, but her eyes widened when she saw Jimmy. "And who's this love?"

"Mrs. White, this is my son, James Lavery."

"You can call me Jimmy," he said, sitting in a chair at the servants' table.

"Well, you're welcome, Jimmy. Are you hungry?"

"A little."

"Of course you're hungry. A growing boy like you. Let me get you some bread and soup."

"Jimmy, I'll be right back," Bridget told him. "I want to check on something."

She ran upstairs and into the drawing room, where girls were sitting about, either studying or doing needlework or practicing picking locks. Bridget leaned inside and gestured to Valérie. The two ladies stepped outside. Bridget couldn't help peeking through the windows, where darkness was rapidly falling.

"Did you find him?" Valérie asked.

"He's in the kitchens."

"Oh, I want to meet him!"

"You should. Has anyone come looking for me?"

Valérie shook her head. "If someone does come, your bags are ready to go. Are you really going to Canada?"

"I don't know. I hope so. I left Caleb fighting off four men. I don't know what's happened to him."

Valérie took her hand. "Surely if any man can escape, it is he."

Bridget prayed that was true.

Caleb felt the rope give. His shoulders burned, and sweat dripped from his forehead. He'd dropped the knife more times than he could count, but finally he'd made progress. He yanked on the ropes, fraying them further, then slipped one hand free. He brought both hands to his chest, wincing in pain as numb muscles came awake again. He wanted to run out of the house as soon as possible, but he forced himself to wait until his arms ceased shaking and he had control of them again.

Caleb went to the window, pulled the curtains aside, and looked out into a dark lane. He tried lifting the window, but it was sealed shut. He'd have to break the glass. The problem was that in doing so he would alert his captors. He hadn't heard them since they'd locked him in, but that didn't mean they'd left the house.

Taking the knife in his hand, he stepped back and rammed the window's glass with his boot. The thick glass cracked but didn't break, and he rammed it again. This time, it shattered. Caleb ignored the sound of footsteps rushing toward the room, clearing the glass and punching out more until he could fit through. When he heard the key in the door's lock, he stood behind the door.

One of his captors crashed through. Caleb jumped on his back and wrestled him to the floor. He slammed the man's head into the wood until he stopped fighting, then Caleb was on his feet again. No others came.

Caleb looked at the knife and at the man, then slid the knife back into his boot. He'd done enough killing for one lifetime.

He wiggled through the window and began to run for Marylebone.

Bridget rose from the kitchen table where she and Jimmy were looking at pictures in a book. She heard footsteps on the stairs, and her heart pounded. But it was only Valérie.

"Still no one?"

"I'm sorry," Valérie said.

"The girls have all gone to their rooms. It is too late to walk through Covent Garden. Stay here with me tonight. We can share my bed, and Jimmy can have your old one." She smiled at Jimmy.

Bridget looked at her son and saw his eyes droop as he stifled a yawn. "You're right." She gathered Jimmy and followed Valérie out of the kitchen. It felt like a betrayal to go to bed. It felt like leaving Caleb all over again. She'd tuck Jimmy into bed, and once he was asleep, she'd come back down. She wouldn't be able to sleep anyway. She was far too worried.

But as they started up the stairwell to the upper floors, someone pounded on the door. Everyone jumped, and then Valérie and Bridget locked eyes. "Take him upstairs," Bridget said as one of the footmen moved to open the door. Bridget stood back. She prayed it was Caleb, but she couldn't be certain one of the men after him hadn't searched for her and found her.

"How may I help you?" the footman asked whomever had knocked.

"I'm here to see Bridget Lavery."

Bridget didn't wait for the footman to respond. She pushed him aside and ran into Caleb's arms. "I thought I'd never see you again," she cried, pressing her face against his shoulder. He was really there, solid and strong and in her arms.

"I managed to escape."

"I was so worried."

"I was worried about you. I—" His body stiffened. "Is that him?"

Bridget turned to see Jimmy on the stairs. "Yes. Jimmy, this is your father, Caleb Harris."

Jimmy stood for a long moment, then rushed down the stairs and threw himself into both of his parents' arms.

It hadn't taken long for the soft rocking of the sea and the sound of waves lapping against the ship to lull Jimmy to sleep. Caleb had sat beside his son, one hand on the boy's chest and the other holding Bridget's hand. It was a bit chilly on the deck, but they'd all huddle together and be warm enough under their blankets.

Bridget rose and went to the railing, and after another long look at his son, Caleb followed. "I can hardly believe he's mine. I don't know what I did to deserve so much good fortune."

"We're both fortunate," she said, leaning against him. "Fortunate to have found each other again, fortunate to have found Jimmy."

"Fortunate to be starting a new life. Are you sorry to leave London behind?"

"A little. Are you?"

"Not in the least. You're my home, Bridget, and I'll be happy wherever you are."

She put her arms around his neck and kissed him, and indeed, he was home.

## About Shana Galen

Shana Galen is a three-time Rita award nominee and the bestselling author of passionate Regency romps. "The road to happily-ever-after is intense, conflicted, suspenseful and fun," and *RT Bookreviews* calls her books "lighthearted yet poignant, humorous yet touching." She taught English at the middle and high school level off and on for eleven years. Most of those years were spent working in Houston's inner city. Now she writes full time, surrounded by three cats and one spoiled dog. She's happily married and has a daughter who is most definitely a romance heroine in the making.

Would you like exclusive content, book news, and a chance to win early copies of Shana's books? Sign up for monthly emails for exclusive news and giveaways at shanagalen.com.

## Books by Shana Galen

If you enjoyed this story, read more from Shana.

**The Scarlet Chronicles** series continues with *Traitor in Her Arms*.

**The Survivors** series begins with *Third Son's a Charm*.

**Covent Garden Cubs** series begins with *Earls Just Want to Have Fun*.

**The Lord and Lady Spy** series begins with *Lord and Lady Spy*.

**The Jewels of the Ton** series begins with *When You Give a Duke a Diamond*.

**The Sons of the Revolution** series begins with *The Making of a Duchess*.

**The Misadventures in Matrimony** series begins with *No Man's Bride*.

**The Regency Spies** Series begins with *While You Were Spying*.

Made in the USA
Lexington, KY
31 October 2018